Braces, Gym Suits, and Early-Morning Seminary:

A Youthquake Survival Manual

Braces, Gym Suits, and Early-Morning Seminary:
A Youthquake Survival Manual

Joni Winn

Covenant Recordings, Inc.
Salt Lake City, Utah

© 1985 Covenant Communications, Inc.
All Rights Reserved
Printed in the United States of America
Library of Congress Catalog Card Number 85-072490
Joni Winn Hilton
Braces, Gym Suits, and Early-Morning Seminary:
A Youthquake Survival Manual
First Printed in Hard Cover September 1985
Second Printing March 1989
Third Printing November 1989
Fourth Printing June 1990
ISBN Number 1-55503-000-9

To Richie and Brandon

CONTENTS

MYTH 1

Everybody Is
Looking at Me

My name is Louisa May Alcott Ziona Barker, and I have no idea why a mother would give her daughter such a ghastly name. I mean, on the one hand, it's obvious. She read *Little Women* by Louisa May Alcott and had to pay tribute to this supposedly terrific author of questionable disposition, but who still had a better name than most of our ancestors (I know; I've done my genealogy). Anyway, no one in my family was personally acquainted with old Louisa May, and it's probably for the best. We all just assume that she was a dandy gal. As for the Ziona, it was invented when some of my greats were pulling handcarts across the plains. I figure the one who thought of it was probably suffering from some kind of heat stroke that makes you delirious. I mean Ziona? They liked the idea of Zion, and I'm certainly not going to knock Zion. But what is it about Mormon parents who try to force some historical tie-in when they invent a name? All it does is create a future disturbance in the genealogy library when some descendant comes upon their little joke and squeals, "Ziona!? Somebody named their kid *Ziona*?!?!" Then the librarian has to get up and walk over to his computer terminal and tell him to keep it down.

And I won't even begin to tell you the problems it has created for me every time I fill out a form that asks for first, middle, and last names. Think what will happen when I get married! I'm going to refuse to marry anyone whose last name has more than five letters in it. Otherwise I'll never make it through life. And forget monogrammed towels. I mean, just forget it.

Anyway, I come from a long line of Mormons, and we live in California where the climate is grossly overrated. Don't look sadly out your windows at the falling snow in Anchorage or St. Paul and think, "Someday I'll have a convertible and go surfing and sit beneath swaying palms in Santa Monica." Believe me, you'd die of heat suffocation. You might even become so sun stricken that you'd name your kid Agatha Christie or Ernest Hemingway.

My dad does something so incredibly complicated I can't begin to explain it. It has to do with building aircraft, okay? He makes a decent living, although there are a lot of tough times and my mom occasionally wrestles with the idea of going back to work (she was a secretary before they married). I hear her on the phone debating this should-a-mother-work question with her Relief Society buddies. They all want to do what's right, but they all also want a swimming pool and a trip to Bermuda. They know raising kids comes first, but at what point can you consider your kids raised enough so that you can go back to work? And if you need the money—I mean for house payments and things—then isn't it okay? One of Mom's visiting teachers said that the only way she'd consider leaving the home to work is if the alternative were public welfare. I was eavesdropping—okay, I'll admit I was eavesdropping—and I thought to myself: "That's easy for you to say. Your husband is a dentist, and you guys have not one but *two* boats, a commercial-sized refrigerator, and more gardeners puttering around your yard than they hire at the temple grounds."

I did not say this, mind you, I simply thought it. My poor mom: She's torn. I'm the youngest and I'm in the twelfth grade and I've told her, "Look, I can come home to an empty house and not fall apart, Mom. Go ahead and work. You'd enjoy it. Consider me raised."

Then she looks at me with that one eyebrow raised, the way she does when Dad tells a corny joke, and she says, "As long as you insist on keeping up with the latest fashions and spending everything you can on records and mascara, I know I'd never see a penny of it anyway."

"Ho, ho, ho," I usually say, though I know she's absolutely right. What is it about me? I have a compulsion to try every new mascara that comes out onto the market, hoping that maybe *this* one will turn my stubby lashes into long, sweeping Minnie Mouse ones.

As for records, I probably buy less than most of my friends. And as for fashion, good grief, Mom—you want me to look like a duck? A nerd? An untouchable? I mean, I have to look *datable*, don't I?

But I see her point. I do tend to think of extra cash as going wasted. I mean, why have perfectly good money tucked away in a drawer when you can trade it for Michael Jackson, wet-look gloss, and ultra super lash?

So I haven't conquered all my weaknesses. I guess I haven't even conquered an acceptable fraction, if I should die tomorrow. But I'm working on it. And I've decided there are some myths that every teenager should relinquish. I'm not very old, but I'll tell you what I've learned so far.

For one thing, teenagers often think that everybody is looking at them. This is not true, even if your name is Louisa May Alcott Ziona Barker.

I think this myth crops up as soon as we discover that we don't have all the answers in social behavior. We worry that we wear the wrong things; we worry that our hair looks funny or that our face is broken out, that our socks are the wrong color, that our underwear will look different when we go to gym class, that we'll say the wrong thing to that cute guy in English, that we'll some how stick out of the crowd and not fit in.

Every girl who ages from ten to twenty has to accept that she'll make mistakes. She'll say the wrong thing, she'll do the wrong thing, she'll get teased and laughed at occasionally. We just have to pick ourselves up, respond with good humor, and go on. I mean, what else can you do? Sit at the bottom of the stairs you just tumbled down and bawl about it? That's life. We need to remember that everybody has awful times like that. It's part of growing up.

But not everyone is watching us. I've done some pretty dumb things and given some pretty dumb answers to questions in class, but one day as I felt the hot fingers of humiliation creeping up my neck, I sneaked a peek at everyone else, and they were so worried about *themselves* that they didn't even notice what a fool I had been.

I have a friend named Michelle (see?—a nice, normal name like Michelle. Some people have all the luck) who goes through about twenty outfits every time she goes out anywhere and she worries like crazy that she'll wear the same thing she wore last time. But you know what? Nobody remembers what she wore last time because they're all worried about what *they* wore last time!

Anyway, just trust me. Most people are so involved in their own concerns that they don't have the time or interest to scrutinize you. Of course there are always those horrible times when we really blow it and embarrass ourselves. Those are the times when we need to remember that we will not die of embarrassment, as much as we often want to. Really, there have been moments when I have been so utterly humiliated I wished I *could* die, but such mercy was not to be mine and I lived to tell the sad tale. One time a friend of mine—a guy I've dated—came over to study, and when I pulled the chair out for him, my cat had thrown up all over the seat. Tell me about anguish! Tell me about humiliation!

And speaking of dating, when I first began I was a bundle of nerves (still am). I was afraid that whenever a guy called me and I picked up the kitchen phone, my mother would choose that exact moment to loudly rearrange the pots and pans. This fear had deep roots in reality, I might add.

But mostly I worried that my parents would somehow embarrass me in front of the guy. I could just visualize my dad taking on a stern expression and saying, "So! What are your intentions regarding my daughter?" or "Young man, are you an Eagle Scout?" or "Do you get straight A's? Louisa tells me you're brilliant. Define *brilliant*."

It's a wonder I didn't have chronic hives from nervousness that first few months. Bad enough that I worried my folks would humiliate me— but my uncle actually *did*! Uncle Verl came over about ten minutes before my very first date—the first one!—and while I was still pulling curlers out of my hair Doug rang the bell.

Doug Embers was a gorgeous senior, and I was absolutely ecstatic to be going to a dance with him. He was on the football team and had a shiny silver Corvette that he actually earned by working on a ranch in the summers. I so desperately wanted him to like my family.

When the bell rang, Uncle Verl popped up to answer the door. Now I have to tell you about Uncle Verl. He's a high councilor and a strong member of the Church, but he believes you should never miss the opportunity to play a practical joke. He gave the stake president a blow dryer for Christmas, which sounds all right unless you happen to know that our stake president is completely bald. That's Uncle Verl for you. He has a whole comedy routine written up and expects it to be read at his funeral. This is a man who even takes a whoopee cushion to ward dinners.

So he swings open the door and there stands Doug. Uncle Verl can't resist: He pretends to be psychotic. "Ho, ho, ho, come right in, little boy. Tell Santa what you want for Christmas," Uncle Verl says.

Doug blinks. Should he laugh? Should he leave? He smiles hesitantly and comes in. Once in, Uncle Verl begins leaping about on the furniture like a baboon, complete with jungle noises. Doug freezes in place near the front door.

Mom comes out of the kitchen wiping her hands on her apron and asks Doug to sit down. "Don't mind Uncle Verl," she says. "He's just crazy." Only Mom smiles as if Uncle Verl is a perfectly acceptable occurrence. She means *crazy* as in *silly* and *wacky*. But Doug is thinking *crazy* as in drag-'em-off- and-lock-'em-up.

Now Uncle Verl sits down beside Doug and slaps Doug on the knee. He leans right into Doug's face and says, "I used to look like you." Doug leans away, smiling politely but absolutely repelled by Uncle Verl. Probably thinks he's dating one of the Munsters.

"Yep," Uncle Verl goes on. "That was before I had plastic surgery to fix it. You could do the same, y'know."

I can hear all this in the bathroom, and I can *not* get the curlers out of my hair so that I can run into the living room and rescue Doug. The faster I hurry, the more tangled they get.

"They say I got pwoblems," Uncle Verl is saying. "Gweat big pwoblems." Oh, please. Not the Elmer Fudd impersonation.

Finally I rip out the last curler—along with half my scalp—and fly into the living room. Doug bolts out of his chair, and we dash from the house. Uncle Verl hollers from the door, "Y'all come back now, y'hear?"

I want to cry. Doug opens my door, and as he walks around to his own door I say a silent prayer.

"Doug, my uncle isn't really crazy; he just likes to kid around like that and embarrass people," I say.

Doug smiles and looks at me. I can tell he doesn't believe me. How could a normal person act that deranged—and do it so well—if he weren't a little bit addled? And why would he do it?

"You just don't understand about my Uncle Verl," I say.

"Does anyone?" Doug asks.

Another time I was trying on some jeans in a store for both guys and girls, and the dressing room doors only snapped closed with a magnet. When I had the jeans up just past my knees I lost my balance and fell through the door into the store, where there was a huge crowd of the most popular kids at school. And there I was on the carpet, writhing around as if I'm in a straitjacket, trying to worm my way back into the dressing room.

Another time I thought I was home alone and turned the radio on and was trying to sing like Barbra Streisand when four of my friends popped out of my closet to "kidnap" me for a pizza dinner. Of course they all thought my singing sounded like a trash can rolling down a driveway. I could have died. All this because I unwittingly finagled my way onto the school newspaper staff, where all the cheerleaders (who like that kidnapping sort of thing) just happened to be that year.

Sometimes it just doesn't pay to get involved in school. My parents always said, "Join the clubs, get into government, become *involved* in school, and you'll enjoy it more."

So I did it—what did I know? The first chance I had was in the tenth grade, and, in a fit of ambition, I volunteered to give the morning announcements over the intercom. All you had to do was read half a sheet of paper, and I figured it was no big deal. Plus it got me out of homeroom and away from that obnoxious Freddie Greenblatt who liked to sit behind me and snort.

(They used to have Principal Hubert read the announcements, but his nasal whine became the butt of so many comical monologues during assemblies— I mean *everybody* could impersonate this poor man— that they decided to give the students a chance to announce. Principal Hubert went into seclusion like Howard Hughes or somebody and has not been heard from since. Some of us kids think he might have skipped out and gone to Acapulco, where he is growing his fingernails long and selling them to a nail salon in Hong Kong. But that's only an educated guess.)

So for one semester on Tuesdays, it was my turn to announce the science exhibits or the football practice or the parent-teacher conferences, or whatever it was that day. And one day, just as I had always done on previous Tuesdays, I sat down at the microphone a few minutes early to await the day's bulletin. I would often chat with Erica, a junior girl who was really sweet and would help out in the admissions office in the mornings. We'd gotten to be pretty friendly, and she had even come to a couple of Mutual parties, though she wasn't a member.

So this one Tuesday we were sitting there, looking out the windows into the hall, and this absolutely gorgeous guy walked by. I knew who he was—he hung out in the art department, and my artistic friends had told me his name was Chuck. He was, at that time, the complete and total love of my life. His name had found its way onto every note pad in our house and into every silent prayer I offered.

"Look!" I said. "There's that guy I was telling you about—there's Chuck Tracy! See? Isn't he gorgeous?"

"Where? Where, Louisa?" Erica asked.

"Right there, going around the corner!" I said, anxious for Erica to feast her eyes upon this incredible creation of manly wonder.

"I can't see him," Erica said.

"How could you miss that perfect hair? Those incredible shoulders! He's so tan." I sighed and pretended to swoon onto the table, my head hitting the top with a "klunk."

And then, with my eyes near the base of the microphone, I suddenly realized that the little red switch was in the "on" position.

The entire school had heard me swooning over Chuck Tracy!

Tell me I didn't want to die right there and go to any kingdom, however humble. So sure, in fact, was I that Chuck Tracy would sail effortlessly into the celestial kingdom that I wanted to go anywhere *else* and never have to face him again. I thought I would never recover, not in a million years, not in an eternity.

I'll tell you this: It is amazing how a below-average student, like Freddie Greenblatt for example, who claims he can't possibly memorize a line of poetry in his English class, can suddenly commit to memory every word he heard me utter over the intercom and recall them *exactly* at any given moment. Yet dozens of otherwise illiterate dolts were doing this for the duration of the school year.

And listen to this. The stake Mutual was planning a big youth conference, right? *Big.* All the kids were invited, and it started out in the chapel, where they were going to have a short presentation to introduce their "surprise" theme. Sister Rinaldi called me and asked if I'd help.

Well, sure, why not? (Ho—the unsuspecting fool that I was—I didn't even ask what I had to do.) "Wonderful," she said. "All you have to do is raise your hand when we ask, 'Who is the most important person in the church?' and then come up to the microphone with four other kids. We'll give you a short line to say as an answer."

What could be simpler? Of course I agreed to her plan, and why not? They were even going to *answer* it for me! So I arrived early the big night of the youth conference, and the place was already packed. Sister Rinaldi took me aside with four other kids and said, "We want this to seem really spontaneous, so act like it isn't planned, okay?" We said okay. "I'll tell you our surprise theme: It's the importance of the individual."

We nodded. Nothing wrong with individuals.

"Now when we ask who the most important person in the Church is, you'll each file up onto the stand and say, 'I think *I* am the most important person in the Church.' "

Okay. Sounds good. The meeting began. Pretty soon Sister Rinaldi stood up and looked lovingly down into the sea of youthful faces. "Who do you think is the most important person in the Church?" she asked, smiling. "Raise your hand if you think you know."

Naturally my hand and the other four kids' hands shot up. Pretending to be picking us at random, Sister Rinaldi called us up onto the stand to answer "so everyone can hear."

"Okay, Louisa, you tell us who you think is the most important person in the Church."

I walked obediently to the microphone. "I think I am the most important person in the church," I said.

And that is when my life took a permanent turn for the horrendous. A couple of guys in the back hooted, and one of them called out, "Boy, does she think she's God's gift!" Some other kids laughed, and there was nervous nudging and whispering all through the congregation.

My eyes froze open. Wait a minute, I thought, these kids don't know that this was planned! Wait—I can explain! But all my inner anguish was useless because smiling Sister Rinaldi tenderly scooted me aside and called up the next kid.

Well after seeing the spectacular response to *my* answer, no way were the rest of the kids going to paint themselves as the conceited snob that *I* had, and they all turned to traitors, saying "the individual" instead of "me." I couldn't believe it!

And then, instead of rescuing me and saying, "Sorry, kids, this was all a deceitful ploy and I *forced* Louisa to say that; I framed her right here in this chapel," Sister Rinaldi just smiled and thanked us and sent us back to our seats—the others in happy relief and me in total agony.

Did anyone ever believe that I was *told* to say that? No! Did any of those kids ever believe that the whole thing was planned ahead of time? No! Did any of them ever let me forget it? No!

I'll tell *you* about embarrassment.

I hope you realize that I could go on and on, telling you some of the embarrassing things that have happened to me, things that make you feel like everyone will stare at you forever.

But suffice it to say that nothing is ever as embarrassing as you think it is at the time. Not everyone will make gaping a hobby. The anguish fades, and the memory dims. And you will definitely survive it.

MYTH 2

My Popularity in High School Will Determine My Success in Life

First of all, I'm not antipopularity, despite the fact that one might have thought so the day I went to fourth grade wearing my Great-aunt Emma's remedy for what turned out to be an allergy to pineapple.

She'd been staying with us for a week (it seemed like a whole summer) and bossing the entire family around. Dad would chuckle quietly to himself behind the newspaper (I knew he was laughing because I could see the paper shaking) while he'd listen to Aunt Emma telling Mom how to load the dishwasher and how to stack her pans. I could hear Mom riding the edge of impatience as she'd say, "Thank you, Aunt Emma," and then "THANK YOU, Aunt Emma." I was hiding out with Dad and trying not to get "under foot," as Aunt Emma would label me whenever I'd tiptoe into the kitchen.

She's my mom's aunt and the only living member of my grandma's immediate family, so my mom feels a certain obligation to put up with Aunt Emma and even invite her to visit occasionally.

But I want you to know I have the whole thing figured out: My mom, who's the ward genealogy bug, wants information that Aunt Emma has. Aunt Emma, who fakes a poor memory at convenient moments, pretends she can't quite recall whether her Uncle Fremont had two sons or three; but whenever she visits she somehow recalls a detail or two that inches my mom's puzzle just that much closer to

Adam. The way I see it, my mom can't stand to lose her only source, and Aunt Emma knows it. She's got bargaining leverage,and boy does she use it. Just when she thinks she won't get invited back the next year, she suddenly calls and tells us about some new miracle drug she's taking that has improved her memory and she thinks maybe—just maybe—the names of Tilly's step-children are coming back to her.

My mom, eager for any tidbit she can get, caves in and invites Aunt Emma back and puts up with having her kitchen rearranged just so she can correct a date from 1784 to 1783. It's better than a spy movie about the trading of Russian secrets! And you know, a weapon like Great-aunt Emma would have crippled the enemy within minutes. Just send her into their kitchen and they would surrender at once.

At the end of the week, Mom and Dad went on a trip (like prison escapees) to Mexico and left us kids in a sinking ship, alone to survive the cooking and caring of Great-aunt Emma. So naturally when I broke out in a splotchy red rash and cough (which I knew was from my politely eating her fruit ambrosia, which I did against my better judgment since pineapple always does this to me), Great-aunt Emma hauled out her trusty memory, blew the dust off, and recalled the recipe for a mustard and hickory paste that would "cure anything that ails you, Dearie."

Like friends, for example. Believe me, if ever you think you're getting too many friends, just call my Great-aunt Emma and ask for her mustard plaster recipe. Knowing her, she has submitted it to a Relief Society cookbook and somewhere near Orem, Utah, there are probably a dozen Primary kids coughing and choking because of the fumes of this hideous concoction. You slather it onto the victim's chest, then wrap towels around it so that it won't "breathe." (The recipient of this medical marvel cannot breathe either, but Aunt Emma's concern is that the plaster itself remain as airtight as possible.)

It has mustard powder in it, and flour (which molds, you understand), and hickory water. How she got or made hickory water I don't know, and you don't *want* to know. I wouldn't pour it on a cracked sidewalk.

Anyway, I toddled off to school wearing this thing and reeking—I mean *reeking*—like nothing you have ever smelled before.

So it wouldn't surprise me if someone thought I was antipopularity.

But I'm not. I think friends are great, and I think we should try to be kind and well liked and admired. I notice lots of Mormon kids become class officers, cheerleaders, student body presidents, and homecoming queens; and these kids always seem to be the ones who hold onto their standards. (The jack Mormons are usually off in somebody's Toyota getting loaded and laughing at lousy jokes. Truth is, the joke's on *them*.)

But I also notice a lot of kids—not just Mormon kids, but *all* kids—who are bending over backwards trying to be accepted and wear and say and do whatever the crowd dictates. They've stopped leading and started groveling.

I think we need to have our own style and our own way of doing things and then let others follow *us*. And they will. You know why? Because most kids in high school don't yet know what they want to think or who they want to be or how they want to dress. They're waiting for somebody who seems confident to come along, slap them on the back more or less, and say, "Hey, Joe. Here's my style. I think this way, I wear these clothes, I do this, and I don't do that. Why don't you come along?" I mean, basically that's what they're waiting to hear. And they think, Well, here's a person who has a good idea and seems happy and in charge, and so I'd better follow that. And they do.

Believe me, I've seen it a hundred times. All it takes is energy. You just have to step out of the crowd and say, "Hey, I'm not going to hang around 7-11 anymore and waste my life. Period. I think it's dumb, and I'm moving on." And you do. And maybe a couple of kids who are too lazy to follow you will tease and jeer and make remarks. But most of the other kids will watch you and think, "Yeah, she's right. This *is* a big waste of time. I'm going with her."

So it's time we stopped bending just as far as we can to fit what others want. Let's tell them how *we* like things and how Mormons live, then let them bend to us. I'm not saying we should be self-righteous; that's a turnoff. I'm just saying that if we don't like taking drugs, then *they* should realize they have to cut it out if they're going where we're going. If we don't like cheating or lying to our parents or experimenting with sex, then let others realize it and follow along. All you're saying when you adopt their low standards is, "Gee, I'm a nobody and you seem like a somebody, so I guess I'll try to be like you."

What a weak position! Yuck! That's as nauseating as the thought of Great-aunt Emma arriving at your door with mustard in hand. I know what's right, and I know what's wrong; we all do. And I'm tired of hanging around kids who haven't grown up to their age level yet. Any kid in his teens knows what's right; and if he's deliberately picking the wrong movies, the wrong jokes, the wrong behavior, the wrong morals—then he's not for me. I deserve better. And so do you. You really do.

Every one of us is a child of God, and he loves us and wants the best for us—the *best*! We have the right to be just as strong in the gospel as we want, without having to look over our shoulders and make sure we're "crowd approved." I'm so tired of worrying about whether everybody in high school likes me. It's so tiresome. Buying certain clothes, saying certain things, gearing my whole life just to please someone I'm not even that close to. It's silly!

So if they call me a goody-goody or a school girl or whatever other degrading name they invent, I'm just going to yawn. Who cares what they say anyway? I'm big enough to walk through all their stupid teasing and not crumble under it. This isn't grade school anymore.

And besides, if I'm still friendly and warm they won't tease me. They'll only feel offended if I adopt a superior attitude. So if I try to be sweet and kind but still stick to my standards, I'll not only avoid teasing but I'll attract even more friends than ever. Kids are looking for somebody strong to follow. Mormons can be the leaders. Why not?

If you don't think kids are looking to follow anybody who seems confident, try an experiment like I did. One day I went to school with my running shoes tied backwards. I mean, I relaced them and put the bow toward the toe. Do you realize that within two weeks every girl at school was tying her shoes like that? It was the current fad! Nevermind that it takes about five times as long to get in or out of your shoes when you tie them this way. Nevermind that this method of lacing has absolutely no redeeming value whatsoever. It was unusual, and I acted confident, as if this were the latest trend, and everybody jumped onto the bandwagon.

Another time I lost an earring in the gym showers and had to go the rest of the day wearing only one earring. Guess what happened within two weeks? You got it.

Once we establish the fact that we blaze our own trail, people will watch us and wait to see what new dictates we're going to invent for them. You'll be seen as someone who has her own personal style, and people will be clamoring to copy you. This goes for morals as well as for fashions.

I know some kids who are really popular—I mean the *tops*. They're good kids and they keep their standards and everything, but maybe they're a little arrogant and try to social climb a little bit. They aren't looking ahead. They think they will be head cheerleader forever. Can't you just see it in the next life? All of us will be standing there in white, but one of us will be carrying pom-poms and shouting, "Whom-Do-We-Appreciate?" (I'm assuming they'll make her clean up her grammar before they let her in, but you never know.)

And maybe she'll be followed by the team captain, who also thought he would be the big man on campus forever, and he'll be mumbling, "82-5-17- hike!" The rest of us will look at him sympathetically and shake our heads. As he passes someone will whisper, "Poor John. High school homecoming was *the event* of his life."

I guess the point I'm making is that being popular in high school is good and it's fun and it can even be a missionary opportunity. But it is, after all, *high school*. It isn't real life. High school ends, and we all go on to college, careers, marriages, missions, families, military—a hundred different destinations. Some people even go *years* without thinking about high school or who the head song leader was.

In my school, it may surprise you, I'm one of the more popular kids. Thanks to my dad, who makes the world's most terrific campaign posters, I've even held school offices; and I'm in several clubs and societies (*not* involving morning intercom announcements, however). But I don't for a minute get a swelled head over any of this and think that when I'm twenty- seven and looking for work after my husband gets laid off (hey, it could happen), I'm going to sit across from a personnel director and say, "But in high school I was vice-president of . . ." She'll laugh in my face. The job market is competitive, and most of those people couldn't care less if you were Paula Popular or Harry Unheard-of. It just doesn't matter after you graduate.

Look at the people who have "made it" in different areas of life: people who really have it together spiritually and have Christ-centered lives and are good Christians and even like their Great-aunt Emmas; people who achieve career goals and would be considered "successful" in the worldly sense; people who are busy giving to others and raising kids and donating to charities and supporting good candidates and really making the world a better place; people who have overcome handicaps and have great attitudes and are even reaching out to help others; people who are famous but who are using that fame to spread good. Think of all the people you might admire. Now how many of these were high school big shots? Think about it. I'm not saying the answer will be zero. I can think of some executive friends of my dad's who are super wealthy but also humble guys, and a couple of them were star athletes and student government gurus when they were in high school.

But just being popular in high school doesn't ensure that you'll sail through the rest of your life without any snags. I want to warn you not to sit back and think that just because you were pretty enough to be "Valentine Sweetheart" that now your life's happiness is certain.

A year from now—certainly five years after you graduate—few people are going to remember or care about your high school victories. Nobody will remember the score of that fantastic game starring *you*, and nobody will recall that when the mayor visited your home ec class it was *your* cherry cobbler he admired. Okay, maybe your mother will remember. But it won't be your ticket to ease. You'll still have to work and study and pray and apply energy to make your life the fantastic experience it can and should be.

I'm not saying it's useless to get involved in high school or to make friends that you'll only be leaving soon anyway; I'm just saying don't put so much emphasis on it that you go all through your teens without ever developing your *self* or getting close to Heavenly Father. Too many kids try desperately to play all the social ego games, only to find later that they were polishing and buffing a public image that, when examined closely, is hollow.

Okay, that's my advice for you popular ones. Now for the 99.9 percent of the rest of you— relax. Like I said, being popular in high school doesn't mean everything. And failing to be the cutest, richest, most flirtatious, most athletic, best-dressed co-ed doesn't mean you'll never see the sun again. Plenty of people blossom late (and then bloom longer), and plenty of other people blossom all the time—only nobody in high school notices it.

I was in the cafeteria once, sitting there with my tray full of who-knows- what (they always serve who-knows-what). I had a cold and was feeling achy and rotten and not even like smiling, let alone laughing. I glanced up from my Kleenex at Ranelle Chasings. (Ranelle's mom probably pulled another one of those rural name tricks on her; it's probably a combination of Ray and Nell or something.)

Anyway, Ranelle was dressed to kill in this totally darling outfit, and she was surrounded by the cutest guys who I'm sure have ever attended our school. She was giggling and winking and flirting and being loud and raucous and licking her lips suggestively and sidling up to the different guys. And they were all laughing and loving it.

I sat there with my red nose and watery eyes and thought, "Louisa, you are looking into a new dimension. You will never visit this dimension; you will never know what it feels like to have that much attention, that much command, that much popularity. Whatever she is saying is far more clever than anything that will ever occur to you, so just look and then blow your nose and go to class."

So I got up and took the long way over to the tray return. (I didn't want to walk right by Miss Life of the Party and look like the before and after of a charm course ad.) And by the time I got there (I stopped to admit to four people that I did in fact feel as lousy as I looked), some of the guys from Ranelle's group were there, too. I cringed. But then my ears perked up.

"Okay, Marc—I'll take the redhead; you take the airhead."

"Hey, forget it, man. You think I'm taking Ranelle? Gimme a break!"

Then they started making fun of her and mimicking her. I was shocked! They had seen right through her phony act! No guy wanted to date a girl who was flirting with every other guy at the school. Sure, they didn't mind laughing in a group, but nobody wanted to put out money for dinner and a movie just to belong to her nameless crowd of a zillion guys.

I felt my cold getting better already. So if you're the brainy computer whiz who gets teased because you bring a copy of *Microcomputing* to class, just smile. You can wave to them from a parade float someday after they ask you to be grand marshall. After all, you'll be founder and president of XYZ Computers, which will be bigger than IBM and Apple put together.

If you're a plain and soft-spoken wallflower who doesn't electrify the room like some of the bouncy girls with plugged-in personalities, just smile. You can pat them on the head someday (or their babies) as you and your husband (who was looking for a strong, supportive, articulate companion) hit the campaign trail for president.

If you're not the smartest kid in class but you're sincere and kind and always try your best—even if everyone teases you for always having the wrong answers—just smile. You can bump into them at the doctor's office someday when you're taking your happy, darling babies for a checkup—and they'll be there for stress reduction and ulcer medication.

If you're the average-looking, average-thinking, average- achieving student, and everyone seems to be buzzing around the kids with money, looks, or other enticements, just smile. You can surprise these socialites ten years later at a class reunion and watch their eyes grow round as they say, "But Melissa! Where did you come from? I never noticed you in high school!" Meanwhile, you will have had to work to get the goodies in life, and you'll have developed habits they never had to. When the tests came, you will have sailed through job difficulties, marital trouble, child-rearing problems—the works. You'll be standing there, a glowing and poised image of the ideal woman, while the former socialite might be anorexic or alcoholic, trying desperately to recapture the popularity that once seemed so easy.

If you're the only one in bed by midnight and the only one without a hangover or fried brains on Monday morning and everybody's teasing you about being afraid to try drugs or to drink, just smile. You can buy one of their pencils someday, as you're stepping over them to get into Saks Fifth Avenue.

Whoever you are and whatever your position is, enjoy it and love being you. There's a plus to your personality whether you're introverted or extroverted, whether you're athletic or studious, whether you're tall or short, whether you're pretty or plain, whether you're popular or unpopular. There is no *right* way to be when it comes to some personality traits.

Maybe, without even trying, you've discovered you're popular (and that is almost always the way it happens). This is as much a responsibility as it is a fun freebie. When people look to us for leadership, we have a special obligation as Mormons to provide the very best—the highest standards, the finest ideals. People who are blessed with many friends and admirers have an especially difficult job: to return that affection sincerely and to leave each of those many lives a little better.

I'd like to see every Mormon kid in the world be popular during high school, *but with the knowledge that it's not crucial to life.* For one thing, it makes life easier to be popular than to wonder why people don't like you and to have to work on the reasons why. But also I'd simply like to see more Mormons in prominent positions, showing the world that it pays off to have high standards and that when we live our religion, good things happen

So if you promise you won't go hog wild and chase fame and acceptance so fast that you make a fool of yourself, I'll tell you what I know about how to be popular and have lots of friends and *good* friends. (By the way, having a few *good* friends is a million times better than having a hundred superficial ones.)

1. Don't gossip. No matter what, don't gossip. Just don't. It always gets back to the person in mention, it hurts incredibly, it's usually filled with falsehoods, it makes you look very bad, and it tells people that when *they're* not there, you're talking about *them.*

2. If you hear gossip about yourself, don't worry about it. People don't talk about the uninteresting folks. They usually talk about the kids who are accomplishing something and of whom they're jealous. Live your life right, and your actions will quickly disprove their words.

3. Be interested in others. Don't be so wrapped up in yourself that you can't think of anything to say. All you have to do is ask a question about the other person—his feelings, his family, his interests, his opinions, his experiences. When you're genuinely interested in somebody else, shyness disappears like magic.

4. Be interesting yourself. You'll find others will be asking *you* questions if you try to learn a little about a lot of things. Study a

language, a sport, a musical instrument, a political issue. Learn to cook, repair a car, hang wallpaper, do CPR, paint with oils, bait your own hook, design a dress, grow an azalea, sing a song, program a computer, write a poem, install a solar panel, understand the stock market, build a birdhouse, put up jam, analyze a best-selling book, get to know a Book of Mormon character, train a dog, do a high dive, enjoy an opera or ballet, tell a funny joke, listen to others. When you dabble in a lot of things, you discover what you're good at; and this feeling of confidence makes you a better leader.

5. Keep your word. If you promise to do something, don't let others down. Don't be late and don't make up wild excuses for yourself, or you'll become known as a flake. "I wonder what crazy story she'll have this time," people will say. You must be dependable and reliable

6. Look for the good around you—in others, in nature, in the world in general—and then point it out. Say, "Look at those great flowers! Have you ever seen anything like that?" Show your love of life in the way you observe and speak. Particularly with others, praise that which is praiseworthy. It says it right in the Thirteenth Article of Faith that "we seek after these things." When you see somebody doing something wonderful, or looking especially vibrant or making you feel especially happy, say so.

7. Think a lot, but say little. This is probably my hardest advice to swallow. I usually tend to blabber on a lot, then think a little and much later. But I've learned that things go much better when I can keep my criticisms to myself and when I wait to speak until others are finished (I tend to interrupt a lot). I notice that when I speak only occasionally, everybody listens, and what I say seems to carry more weight.

8. Really care about others and look for opportunities to do favors and good deeds. Seriously, keep a record and promise yourself every day that you will do three *secret* nice things for someone. If you get found out, it doesn't count. You'll be surprised how good you will feel. And you'll find yourself doing other deeds, too, like opening doors for people, helping someone who's carrying a million books, cheering up people who seem down. This is a good one and wins you lots of friends very quickly.

9. Be a good sport. Have a sense of humor, even when you're being teased. Don't get all huffy and serious over every little thing. If everybody wants to peel off their socks and go wading, don't be a big baby about it. If you want to go shopping and the others decide to head for the beach, be a sport and go along. Be someone fun to be with, not

the disagreeable one who's always whining, "but I wanted to go to the movies instead of this dumb restaurant."

10. Be flexible, open, and breezy. Don't get into heated arguments and battles over silly things. (Most subjects which arise in high school are, looking back, pretty silly.) Don't be panicky, hard-headed, or difficult. Respect other people's ideas and opinions and be open to change yours. Be firm about morals (you leave your mind *wide* open and pretty soon people start dumping garbage into the ravine). But don't be rigid about things unrelated to the gospel.

11. Be warm. More than any other trait, I think warmth is the key to having friends. If you make everyone around you feel as though you really enjoy them and care about them, people will gravitate to you like you're the latest fragrance. I mean it! You want to project an image that doesn't judge, doesn't condemn: "Come in and relax. Kick your shoes off. I don't mind. I like your company, and in my house you're always welcome." That kind of warmth makes anybody feel special.

12. Seek friends from a variety of areas. Look for people who have widely differing interests. The wrestling champ, the clarinet player, the drama queen, the economics wizard, the model, the office assistant— they may not have anything in common with each other, but they can each have something in common with you. Your life will be richer and more well rounded if you try to vary the opinions and feelings you're exposed to. If all your friends feel, look, act, and talk just the way you do, you might as well live in a house of mirrors. You won't grow or develop properly if you're surrounded by such a narcissistic collection of yes-men. Put some spice into your life, and learn something new!

13. Don't hold grudges. Let Heavenly Father do the judging. It's a miserable job, but he evidently wants it so why not let him have it? If we judge a sinner, he's told us, our sin is worse! Good grief, who needs that? Plus, if you've never had the chance to forgive someone who has really done you wrong, you don't know how good it feels. It feels like your chest is full of tiny, bright helium balloons. It feels airy and light and wonderful!

And anyway, it's a lot of work to nurse a grudge. I learned this at Michelle's house one night when we were helping out with her little sister Amy's slumber party. The girls had popped popcorn and played with makeup and had pillow fights and worn themselves to exhaustion leaping around to a music videotape. Finally they crawled into their sleeping bags and began the female ritual of talking well into the night.

Michelle and I tiptoed down to check on them, and we could hear some of the girls still talking. The conversation had taken a sour turn, and two of the girls were criticizing another girl who wasn't there, Jenny Foster.

"I can't stand the way she brushes her hair," one said.

"Oh, I know. And she's always trying to boss everybody around."

They went on and on, picking Jenny to pieces. Finally one of them said, "Hey, Amy, don't you think Jenny Foster looks like E.T.?"

There was some giggling, then a sleepy voice came from across the room, "Huh? Oh, I'm too tired to hate Jenny Foster anymore." With that, Amy konked out and the others decided to call it a night, too.

I thought about that simple incident for a long time and about the trouble and energy it takes to dislike someone. Sweet little Amy really hit it right on the head: It's too tiring to hold a grudge. It wears us out and keeps us from thinking thoughts which make us happy, thoughts which help us to grow.

We have to forgive and forget. If we don't forget, we haven't truly forgiven. Whenever I catch myself ruminating about some rude person I've met or some offensive thing someone has done, I decide that here is where I will apply the laziness that Mom won't let me keep in the house. If I'm going to take the easy way out of something, I'll let it be hating. I'll decide that it's just too much trouble to work myself into a sweat over someone who doesn't deserve that much of my energy. Then I'll sigh and maybe doze off and wake up smiling. Want to procrastinate? Put off holding grudges.

14. Don't abandon your friends when they're down. If someone you know makes a mistake or does something stupid and is suddenly teased or ostracized by the other kids, you be the one to reach out and offer friendship. That's when they need it the very most. Sometimes the reason a girl will get into drugs or into a rough crowd is because that's the only place where she feels accepted.

15. Give; don't lend. More friendships are broken up over this than almost anything I can think of. Someone asks to borrow twenty dollars and you lend it to them. A few days go by and still the friend hasn't paid you back. You begin to resent it. The friend, feeling guilty, begins to avoid you. Pretty soon you're finding fault and fostering bad feelings toward one another.

My dad and mom have always told me, "When someone wants to borrow something, offer to give it to them. If you cannot afford to lose it, don't give it at all."

I've really lived by that. If a friend wants to borrow a book or a scarf or some money, I think to myself, "Can I bear to part with this— permanently?" And if I can, I enjoy being generous and giving it to them without any obligation imposed for its return. That way the heat's off, and they can face you without guilt. You can also face them knowing they are not in your debt; they simply accepted a gift.

A girl at school asked to borrow some money from me once, and I explained my policy. "Lisa," I said, "I can spare the five dollars right now. You can have it, and please don't worry about ever paying me back. Just forget about it, okay?"

She was really surprised and grateful, but you know what? The next Monday she handed me the full amount. The result was that Lisa felt good about herself, yet not as though I were cracking the whip. We stayed friends, and from my standpoint it was simply a pleasant— and very unexpected—surprise when she paid me back.

(Not only that, you don't have to do any mental bookkeeping to keep straight who owes you what! See? There's always a practical advantage!)

If you follow all these guidelines, I promise you'll have plenty of friends, and I mean the kind of close friends you'll keep your whole life. But you might never be voted Most Personality, and when you consider what some high school kids admire, you might not want their esteem. If you really and truly like yourself, it won't matter how many phone calls you get in a week.

I remember a couple of years ago, when I was just starting high school, I was too dressed up the first day and a bunch of guys teased me about "new school clothes." I could have died. I mean, what can you do about it? There you are all pressed and crisp and looking like it's the first day of school, and there they are pointing it out. You can't change your clothes, and even if you could, that would be admitting they were right.

I remember I went home from school and burst into tears. Mom rubbed my back, and Dad came over and asked me what happened. I told them the whole ugly story—my hideous experience at the hands of my ruthless fellow students. I really poured it on. Bless their hearts, they didn't even laugh. (I have to hand it to them, there. If I had a little sister and she came home wailing about something so trivial as that, I'd tease her to death.)

Anyway, Mom said it only meant the boys liked me. (What can you expect from someone whose favorite book is *Little Women?*) I stared at her as though she had just announced that she was going to run away and become a yacht racer.

"What are you talking about?" I moaned.

She said when boys want to talk with a girl but don't know what to say, they tease her. She said to consider myself lucky.

I looked over to Dad in hopes of appealing to reason. Surely he would understand that what I had just experienced was anything but luck.

And then you know what? He actually agreed with her and said he remembered doing the same sort of thing when he was that age and even when he met Mom! (How could she marry someone who initially acted so immature? She must have had X-ray vision, and been able to see through his sophomoric antics, knowing a stable, well-adjusted father was hiding in there somewhere.)

Then Dad told me something I've often enjoyed thinking about. He told me not to worry about being popular with the big football heroes. "Dating a football hero is easily less important than, say, ice cream," he said. I giggled; what was he getting at?

"And let's face it. If you really had to, you know you could live without ice cream. When it comes to importance, ice cream just isn't that high up there," he said. And this, coming from a man who eats a big bowl full of Rocky Road four nights a week. "So if it's less important than ice cream and even ice cream isn't that important, you know it's not worth worrying about, right?"

I laughed. I was so tired I couldn't tell if he was being logical or not. But it sounded good and reminded us both that there was still a half carton of Rocky Road in the freezer.

We finished it off in the porch swing.

MYTH 3

If I Can't Look like a Movie Star, Life Isn't Worth Living

Well, if this were true we'd all be dead, wouldn't we? Yet so many of us honestly believe that we can never be happy unless we stop traffic and cause a few collisions, even when we're in a robe and curlers. We really expect so much of ourselves and place so much importance on appearance.

I heard about a recent poll taken among some high school kids, asking who they would most like to be. I couldn't believe some of the answers: *all movie stars!* Do that many of us think fame and fortune equals happiness? Would we really want the minds and hearts of total strangers? ("Well, no," says my friend Kelly Matheson, "but how about just their faces and figures?")

We think good looks will be the answer to everything. It's wrong, and I'm so glad I know it while I'm still young. Think of the money I'll save at the plastic surgeon's office! Think of the anguish I'll save when I make hopeless comparisons between myself and someone who has the current "look."

Okay, I'm not free from doing that. I still look at others and envy certain things or sigh because I don't measure up in some way. But a little of that is healthy: it motivates me to get into shape and to keep up with grooming and to challenge myself so I'll continue to grow and learn. That's all right.

But what's wrong is to put looks at the top of the list and then live for that. And to believe that if we can't be on the cover of *Vogue* we belong in a dog kennel. A healthy interest in our appearance is good, but taking it to the extreme leads to vanity, anorexia, phoniness, and greed.

Olivia Kay Burtell spends hours—I mean hours—blow drying her hair so it will feather just the right way. She puts on mascara one eyelash at a time, then still separates each lash with a needle when she's through. She takes forty-five minutes to get ready for bed and spends an incredible amount of money on cosmetics. Now we're talking about a town where I live— I go a little overboard on mascara (but I slop it on fast)—so it's hard for me to learn this, too. But while I live on the outskirts of this disease, *this* girl lives in the heart and soul of it. When you hear statistics about how many billions of dollars are spent in the United States on cosmetics, I always wonder why they don't say, "in large part by Olivia Kay Burtell." I'm serious—it looks like she puts her base coat on with a putty knife. Everyone at school is stunned at the strength she must have in her neck to support the weight of it all. Poor Olivia. She's so used to seeing herself overly made-up that to try getting by with less must look bare and pale to her.

And I feel sorry for her. She's where I would be without the gospel, probably. If I didn't know the dangers of vanity and the importance of inner beauty, I might be chasing an image just as fast and as furiously as Olivia does.

There's another girl at school, Kimberly Scott, who always wears the wildest clothes you have ever seen. I mean, when the punk rocker and the purple mohawk and the Boy George and the unisex looks were in, Kim followed full throttle. Every month her hair was a new blaze of color and pattern, buzzed here and braided there. Her face was painted like a Modigliani painting, and her clothes looked like rejects from the Russian circus.

I remember one time I went over to Lyndsey Kramer's house to work on a science project while Lyndsey's little sister, Cara, was upstairs playing dress-ups. We had just sat down at the kitchen table with our Seven-Ups and our homework when the doorbell rang.

It was Kim. She had on some neon blue pants with pink paint splattered on them, a yellow pirate's shirt, red spike heels, several patchwork scarves, a leopard-print vest, huge black chain necklaces, giant green earrings, a floppy brown hat, and zebra-striped makeup. I tried to gulp quietly as Lyndsey invited her in. (Kim had come to pick up some class notes that Lyndsey had taken for her while she had flown back East to see a rock concert by a group called Metal Breath or Molten Brains. Something like that.)

Everything went fine until Kim was standing in the doorway saying good-bye. Then suddenly Cara came charging down the stairs in her dress-ups. She had thought I was going home and wanted to say good-bye. But instead of good-bye, she said, "Oh, wow—you guys play dress-ups really neat!"

Kim, whose vast array of attributes unfortunately does not include a sense of humor, just glared angrily back at little Cara.

Fortunately (for Cara), Kim's vast array of cosmetic murals *did* include a painted on clown smile, so even though she was frowning it looked as though she were grinning. Cara grinned back.

Lyndsey and I held our breath as we looked back and forth from Cara to Kim. Except for Cara's tiny size, they looked like mirror images of each other.

Cara had on an old pair of red party pumps, bright blue bloomers which hit her spindly little legs at midcalf, a yellow sweat shirt, a fake alligator-skin purse, a polka-dot jacket missing one sleeve, green bubble earrings, and a brown fishing hat with two feather fishhooks stuck in the front. She'd found some red lipstick and smeared it across her lips and cheeks, while some black mascara had been crookedly etched into squiggly stripes from her forehead to her chin.

It was an immediate study in both duplication and in contrast. Here were two people dressed exactly alike but wearing opposite expressions: Kim looked furious and humiliated; Cara looked pleased to pieces, nearly squealing with joy that she'd "done it right."

Lyndsey and I just stood there, completely flabbergasted and embarrassed. Then before Lyndsey could speak (and say what?) Kim snapped, "Very funny, Lyndsey. You sure went to a lot of trouble to have your little joke, didn't you?" Then she left, slamming the door.

Cara blinked her round little eyes. "What happened?" Then Lyndsey and I started giggling; we couldn't help it. We felt bad that Kim was so offended, and at school we repeatedly tried to tell her that we had no way of knowing what she would wear and that even if we had, we wouldn't have dressed Cara up like that. Somehow the wording wasn't right, and Kim only got madder. The harder we tried to apologize, the deeper the hole we dug.

So we finally decided to fall back upon our initial reaction, which was to view the event as one of the singularly hilarious coincidences of the modern era.

It also taught me not to dress like a fool, lest I be thought one.

We don't have to rebel against everything sensible to have our own individuality, you know. Being independent is not the same thing as bucking the system just to be outrageous.

I'll tell you how I learned to have my own look and my own style. It was from going camping. My dad and my brothers decided with two other families to go on a backpacking trip. They thought (being the lousy cooks that they are) that it would be fun to bring the women along this time. My sister Barbara had just gotten married and gone on a honeymoon to a nice, clean, air-conditioned complex with jacuzzis and tennis courts. Some people have all the luck. As for Mom and me, we remained to pack up our cookware and mosquito repellant and act enthusiastic about "roughing it." I'd say we did a pretty good job. I did a better job than she did, of course, since I was considered a little kid who was too frail to carry very much.

Finally, like a team of pack mules, we arrived at the camp site sweating and aching. The men were all raving about how great it was. The women were all gasping for breath and looking at each other with crossed eyes.

At first the women all tried to keep up their appearances. Some of the girls had brought along makeup kits disguised as fishing tackle boxes, and while the guys were puttering around with their Swiss army knives and mess kits, the girls were behind a tent with their magnifying mirrors, plucking their eyebrows and dusting their cheeks with Melt-Me-Mauve.

Three days later we'd survived a mud slide, a horned owl invasion, a cloud burst, a heat wave, starvation, and poison oak. Makeup was the *last* thing on my mind. I noticed some of the women were getting up and splashing cold water on their faces from a stream. Their cheeks were rosy without any help, and their eyes sparkled with the humor you had to have to survive. Their skin seemed tighter and smoother (maybe we were all losing too much weight!), and their hair fell in soft, natural curves. Suddenly it hit me that everybody was getting prettier. Makeup has its benefits—I mean there are times you want to look glamorous with smoldering eyes and frosty-tinted lips—but that's an artificial beauty. What I was seeing on this camping trip was the inner beauty shining out from the inside. No camouflage, no pretense. It was great!

And then I knew it wasn't my imagination, because I overheard some of the young guys talking with my brothers. They were all commenting on how smart they were to bring the prettiest girls around. How blue someone's eyes were, how cute someone's smile. They loved seeing their wives and girl friends without makeup! Sure, they don't want their wives looking like prospectors with picks and shovels, but they liked the natural, fresh glow that gave them a new kind of appeal: an outdoorsy, uninhibited honesty.

And none of us had perfect features—not by a long shot. If analyzed for a beauty magazine, I'm sure we'd be criticized for our high foreheads, sparse eyebrows, thin lips, fat cheeks, big noses, and all the rest. Yet because we finally learned that it's who we are inside that counts—and because we were forced to abandon our cosmetic crutches—we felt prettier than ever, and it showed on our faces.

Our posture seemed better, our steps were livelier (they had to be or you'd break your ankle), and we felt more energy and joy. Energy and joy are two things you just can't conceal; they shine forth like beacons and *that* is beautiful.

There are still times when I forget that inner beauty is most important. Sometimes I feel like I will never be my ideal weight and my hair will never have the body it needs and my brown eyes will never truly sparkle. But I make the most of what I have and play all the fashion and makeup tricks to hide the less desirable and to emphasize the positive. I try not to follow fads, and I buy clothes that are classic, clothes that flatter *me* regardless of the latest trend.

I use makeup to highlight what already exists, rather than paint on a stranger's face from a magazine. I stay moderate, just adding extra sparkle or deeper shades for evening.

I do diet and strenuously, not only for appearance but for health. The Word of Wisdom is probably disobeyed more in the area of obesity than in any other way, and I don't want to be considered "a fat Mormon girl." I don't even want to be chunky. I want to have enough meat on my bones so people don't constantly point out how skinny I am, yet little enough so that I'll look good in my clothes and won't have to cringe about out-of-proportion bulges. I want to have pep and vigor, and you can't have that if you're terribly underweight or overweight.

I remember always that hygiene is basic, and I pamper myself with cleanliness, including Mr. Bubble. Say what you will about rubber ducks and bubble bath, they're a permanent part of my life. When I get married and have children, I fully intend to continue luxuriating in baths full of toys and suds. I will always wear a Mickey Mouse hat when I go to Disneyland, too. Certain elements of childhood should never be abandoned.

And that's part of it, right there. I mean, it really is. *Attitude.* I *think* of myself as pretty adorable at times, if I must say so myself. I have weaknesses, sure, tons of them. But I like me and I like my body and I like my face. A sculptor could go over it and pick it to pieces making improvements, but it's *my* face and *my* self and I like it. I'll try to make the best of myself and keep myself looking good, but I'm not going to be self-critical anymore. I'm too much fun and too good to me for that. Seriously! Who else would treat me to a new hairdo, just for finishing my homework early? Who else would let me indulge in a hot fudge sundae just for doing the dinner dishes? Who else would allow me a whole day of playing in the park with some cute little kids and puppies, just for studying my scriptures?

I give myself rewards because I deserve my own love. We all do. I push myself to the limit sometimes, too, and I demand an awful lot of myself at school and elsewhere. But I remember that I like myself and I like my looks and who I am.

Matter of fact, I think that observation calls for a bubble bath.

MYTH 4

If I Let People Know I Have a Testimony, They'll Think I'm Weird

I discovered this myth when a friend took the big, bold leap and just suddenly stood up in church one day and bore the most beautiful testimony I'd ever heard. She talked about how her dad gave a blessing to her brother and it healed him, and she talked about prayer and how she even prayed about the same crazy little things I pray about and how Heavenly Father did listen to her. She admitted that she didn't always act like it but that she really loved her parents and she also knew that Joseph Smith was a prophet and she had gotten her witness during a sacrament meeting.

I remember holding my breath as she was talking, afraid I'd start crying. It was so strange: I felt really proud of her. I wanted to pop! Everything she said sounded so true and so sincere.

I didn't have the courage that Sunday to stand up and echo what she'd said, but the next month I prayed really hard for the strength to swallow my pride and admit what I honestly felt. And suddenly the microphone was in my hand and it was easy! It felt so good to voice what I'd held in secret for so long. Because Heather broke the ice, I knew I could do it without worrying about being teased. I knew it was right, and my testimony actually grew for having borne it.

Nobody made fun of me. Nobody laughed. Instead, everyone just reacted the same way I had when Heather had borne her testimony. They all just breathed a big sigh of relief that someone else felt the same way they did. It had gotten (in our ward anyway) so that everybody was trying to be so cool and so tough that nobody dared admit a love of God for fear of being teased. In class if you answered a question right, the others would accuse you of being "churchy." I was so glad Heather broke the downward spiral.

Unless we're recent converts to the Church, sometimes we don't even analyze what a testimony is. It's a belief in God, in the plan of salvation, in Jesus as the Christ, in Joseph Smith's vision and restoration of the priesthood, and in the truth of a living prophet today.

Why should we have a testimony? It's a shield and a protection. I know it shields me from all the hassles of daily living. I look at all the craziness around me and then I look at the gospel of Christ, and it reminds me of what really does matter and what's just current trends. It's my anchor and my measuring stick, against which everything I hear must be measured, so I'll know what's right and what's just Mrs. Billingsly spouting off about reincarnation (she's a math teacher who thinks she was a Rockette in an earlier life). We can cling to our testimony when all else is nutso.

A testimony opens doors for revelation and inspiration. It makes us grateful for all our blessings and makes us want to be worthy of them. It advances our personal relationship with the Savior—which is one of the key things we are to acquire while on this earth. It makes us more forgiving and more forgivable. It gives us hope for the future.

To have one we must hunger and thirst for it and want it with great intensity. We can't just lie in bed and think, "Oh, a testimony—yeah, that would be nice." We have to crave it as strongly as we crave oxygen. Sometimes we have to cry thousands of tears before we get one.

If you want a testimony and you don't have one, here's how to get one. Desire, as I just mentioned, has to be there. Then you have to humble yourself and listen to the whisperings of the Spirit. That's sometimes hard to do, especially if you're a good student and you think you're the first intellectual to ever examine the gospel and you have all these theological arguments. To listen to the Spirit you have to realize that we're all mortal and that we may know one or two things, but God knows infinitely more than we do. You also have to realize that you don't attack a testimony the way a detective tackles a mystery. You don't just lay out all the data and analyze it with a slide rule. You pray about it. Hard. You listen to the Spirit, which, by the way, can tell you things far more convincingly than can your eyes or ears or reasoning powers.

In fact, once the Spirit whispers to you, you can't deny it. If you prove a math theorem, you may learn a later law that disproves your theorem and you then willingly abandon that initial belief. This doesn't happen with the Spirit. It only tells us eternal truths, things that don't change. Ever. Our eyes and ears can play tricks on us; worldly philosophies change and get updated; you just can't trust things you can "deduce." But once the Spirit tells you something—Wham! It's solid and it's permanent and it zings through your whole body.

You can't hear the Spirit very well at a rock concert. Oh, I suppose it has happened. But it's rare. And you can't hear it very well at a wild party or when you're blabbing on the phone to a buddy. I've found the best places for hearing it are in church or in quiet scripture study at home. It takes concentration.

And don't expect fireworks. I guess some people get thundering witnesses, but most people just get a quiet warmth deep inside that grows and swells until you almost feel you can't contain it in one small body. It's a comforting, cozy, loving feeling. Like a hug around your heart.

Speaking of scripture study, that's something else you have to do. You have to learn what the gospel is about and what Jesus taught. Along with that goes fasting, and I don't mean just skipping meals. Real fasting starts and ends with prayer and has a specific purpose. You reflect upon what you're fasting about *many* times every hour, praying almost continually and getting as close to God as you can. On Fast Sunday, for example, we should listen all the more intently in our meetings; we should really concentrate on the lyrics of the hymns we sing.

When we pray we shouldn't use memorized phrases. It should pour from our hearts and feel "real." In a Young Women class I remember, our teacher said that when you get the urge to skip prayers, that's when you most need to get down on your knees and do it.

Don't expect a testimony to come all at once or to know everything about the gospel all at once. Heavenly Father feeds us as he sees that we can digest it. He's not going to dump the entire gospel into our souls just because we pray about it one time. He gives us little portions and waits to see how we do with that little bit of knowledge. Then if we can handle that and want more, there's always plenty waiting for us.

But too many people expect too much too soon. They think they don't have a testimony if they don't know the Doctrine and Covenants by heart. They think they have to know the entire history of the

Church, including every item in every handcart, before they can consider themselves true Mormons. All you have to do is have a burning conviction that it's true. That's all. Then the rest comes with study.

I think the biggest stumbling block to getting a testimony is laziness: It sounds like too much trouble. Yet the complainers and the grumblers are the very ones who won't invest the energy it would take to solve their problems and answer their questions. Study of the gospel is essential, and not just until you get a testimony; it's continual.

John A. Widtsoe said, "It is a paradox that men will gladly devote time every day for many years to learn a science or an art; yet will expect to win a knowledge of the gospel, which comprehends all sciences and arts, through perfunctory glances at books or occasional listening to sermons. The gospel should be studied more intensively than any school or college subject. They who pass opinion on the gospel without having given it intimate and careful study are not lovers of truth, and their opinions are worthless."

That sure rings true to me. And last, just as you would purchase or embrace anything, try it on. Try living the gospel—I mean really living it— and see if it doesn't bring you greater joy and happiness. It will, I promise you.

Over one hundred years ago Bishop Orson F. Whitney said that we will be tried to the very core. Leaders have told us to have strong testimonies and not live on borrowed light—or we will fall.

Too many kids put off getting a testimony. Yet the strength which comes from having one is exactly what you need to get through your teen years.

President David O. McKay said a testimony "is the most precious thing in all the world." Why do we procrastinate the development of a strong testimony when it's so very important?

When we're baptized and when we take the sacrament, we promise to be witnesses. We need to bear our testimonies, both privately when we're inspired and in testimony meeting. How do you do that?

Just tell how you feel. Don't worry about form; think about substance. Don't give laundry lists of public thanks, don't give travelogues, don't lecture, and don't meander through pointless stories. Don't blurt out terribly personal and sacred experiences that are too special to be scattered carelessly into any congregation. Just tell what you believe.

Other people can gain tremendously from hearing you bear your testimony. Without knowing it, some little thing you say might be exactly what lifts somebody's heart and gives them the push they need along their path.

You don't have to be a Relief Society president to have a testimony. You don't have to be old either. The Spirit bears witness to people of any position and any age. Even tiny kids can know the Church is true. Sure, they don't know all the details about ordinances and priesthood and such, but they can know how they feel. President Kimball says testimonies come from the heart.

In youth it's especially exciting to be able to bear a testimony because— due to the fact that most kids are afraid to do it—you can be such an outstanding leader. We can and must shine forth— seriously—like bold beacons from the mountaintop, like the two thousand stripling warriors in the Book of Mormon, brave and faith-filled. We must find out that it is true, then let the whole world know what we know.

You realize, of course, that if you don't share the gospel in this life, dozens of your acquaintances will be waiting for you in the next life, probably with their hands on their hips, to hear your feeble excuses. Hey— you might even bump into some crotchety old neighbor who'll chase you down and slap a mustard plaster on your chest.

Take it from me: You're much better off bearing your testimony now.

MYTH 5

Friends Are More Important than Family

I used to look at my friends' families and feel jealous. Why were their parents so good looking, so rich, so understanding? Why were all their brothers and sisters so accomplished and so fun? Why were their houses filled with more good things to eat? And then, on a long bus ride to a youth conference one year, we all got to talking and I found out they all felt the same way about my family and my house! We really laughed. Every one of us had been looking at the inside seams of our own homes and the outside gingerbread on everybody else's—you know? We knew our parents' weaknesses, we were tired of the way our own moms cook, we saw other families that were different, and just because it was new we had assumed it was better. Underneath, their moms scolded them just as much as mine did me. And their brothers teased them just as much and their parents argued just as much and their refrigerators were just as boring. It was good for all of us to have that talk.

In the end I think we all realized just how terrific our families are and how much we have to be thankful for. I felt guilty for having been so critical and unappreciative. My mom really is a good cook—and an adventurous cook—and my folks are well groomed and provide a nice home and my brothers and my sister are even more tolerable than most. I really felt ashamed for having taken so much for granted.

I think back about all the times I have tapped my dinner glass with a spoon and announced, "My brothers are of no use whatsoever." Of course, I only do this when they come home for a visit. "What good are you when I need help in my Spanish class?" I moan. "Bill went to Denmark on his mission, and Darin went to New Zealand. What good is Danish or Maori ever going to do me? Go away."

Then they laugh and continue to eat up all the brownies I made that morning—or macaroons, or lemon bars—whichever recipe had sounded best that day. I always try to make something yummy when Bill and Darin come home, partly so their mouths will be full and I'll get a word in edgewise, and partly because, after all, they're my poor inept brothers who can't fix a bowl of cereal without an instruction manual.

The subject of Bill and Darin came up one night while I was helping Mom with the dishes. "Then men" had settled down to watch a football game. It's always the same.

"Why didn't you teach them to cook?" I ask Mom. "Then they could be bringing me cheesecakes and chocolate eclairs, instead of gobbling up what I make."

She shrugs.

"They're a throwback to the Stone Age," I whine."When I have boys, you better believe they'll learn to cook. What if Bill and Darin can't find anyone who'll marry them—and without cooking skills, it could happen—how will they eat?"

Mom shrugs again. "They just weren't interested."

"Not interested? They're interested in eating, aren't they?" At this point, Dad, who knows I'm right but also knows he doesn't want a new order of full equality established in his house (just yet, anyway), rises from his recliner and comes into the kitchen clearing his throat and acting as if he knows his way around there.

"Now, Louisa," he says, "Bill and Darin know a lot of things you don't know. Your mother is such a good cook no one ever thought of trying to compete with her, that's all."

I see the whole ploy: Make me feel guilty because I don't know how to fill a pill bottle (Bill's going to be a pharmacist) or how to juggle capital gains (Darin's going to be an accountant), and then win Mom over to your side with cheap flattery.

"It's like refusing to teach a kid to make his bed or do laundry or balance a checkbook," I said. "It's a survival skill. And it would also make a little sister very happy if occasionally one of her brothers would return home with a small Boston creme pie."

Dad shakes his head at that point and drifts back to his workshop or TV or magazine. Mom looks at me. "I guess I should have insisted," she says. "But they were so busy with sports and school. It really is a double standard, isn't it?"

You know, the problem with parents agreeing with you is that you never get any practice in the fine art of argumentation and debate. Fwap! There goes the wind right out of my sails.

"Oh, Mom, I'm sorry," I say. "You're a good mother and all. I hadn't meant to put you down. I just guess it bugs me that guys expect women to do everything."

She laughs. "I'm not so enlightened and hope I never have to be," she says. "The day your father makes me mow the lawn or change the oil I think I'll die."

Okay, division of labor. That's fair. So when can I have a car that Bill or Darin will repair? I tell you, life never equals out. And I guess we shouldn't sit and wait for that. I mean, sometimes we end up short and sometimes we get a bonus. It's just the way it goes. In fact, Bill and Darin probably did more for me as I was growing up than I'll ever be able to do for them. So who am I to complain? A sassy kid, I guess.

I have an older sister who's thirty and has four kids. Barbara's pretty neat and doesn't seem that old at all. She understands about boys and school and Mom and Dad. She even knows what I'm talking about when we discuss music or fashions. And three of her four kids are terrific, too. Two boys and a girl. But the oldest girl is a holy terror. That kid needs to be sent on a cruise to Taiwan or someplace. Or at least I need her to be sent on one. Maybe let her come back when she's about thirty-five or so. I never mention it to Barb, but that kid could send you to an early grave. I'm sure Barb and her husband know it and don't need a seventeen-year-old to point it out. That kid flushed an entire carton of eggs down the toilet when she was six years old. She colored the trim on all our lamp shades with magic marker. She pressed Play-Doh into all the electric sockets and poured flour into all the oven burners. She scratched two doors of the station wagon with a toy bracelet, broke seven of my record albums, threw my best shoes into the trash compactor, and broke all Dad's gladiolas in half. And the whole time she's pillaging and plundering like this, she has this sappy little smile on her face. I tell you that kid is not headed for unparalleled popularity.

But maybe she'll outgrow it and turn out to be the best one in the family. That's what my mom is counting on, and since it's about the only thing left you *can* count on, I count on it too.

At family reunions the old folks see her coming and practically dive into bushes to get out of her path. She knocks over the buffet table (four strong men couldn't do this if they tried), and all the food goes flying. Barbecued beans, potato salad, jello salad, hot rolls, Aunt Emma's fruit ambrosia (well, no loss there), lemonade, cookies—the whole works. Then somebody's dog snatches a piece of chicken, and Aunt Betty goes into hysterics screaming about how poultry bones puncture a dog's intestines. Parents grab their toddlers who are meandering over to pick up pieces of broken glass, and Barbara just stands there with this funereal expression on her face, utterly hopeless about how to control her daughter. (Wouldn't it be interesting to send Great-aunt Emma on a long cruise, handcuffed to this kid—and see who surrenders first?)

Otherwise the reunions are great. All my friends hate family reunions, but I love them. I think they're hysterical. I love to watch people panic about unimportant things ("Oh, Wilbur, I told you to bring the honeybutter. Now we'll have to put plain butter on these rolls!") and fight their way through an unfamiliar kitchen. I like watching the cousins get reacquainted and compare freckles. It's fun to see some of the same physical traits as they show up in baby after baby. "Look, that one has Marty's eyebrows, too!"

And I love to watch people trying to get along because it's family and we simply must. That is what I really love.

It would be so easy, if this were a block party or an old army buddy reunion, to think, "I'm not putting up with this. These people are strange and thoughtless and silly." But when it's a family reunion, we have to learn to overlook all these idiosyncracies and faults. We have to look for the good (and sometimes it's a real hunt, let me tell you) because we are sealed to these people and they're our eternal family and they may be great or they may be awful, but they're all we've got.

Again, I'm lucky. I have a lot of relatives who are such good Latter-day Saints and such loving parents and such fun people to be around that seeing them again is a pure joy. I feel fortunate to have role models right within my own family. But, like in every family, there are one or two bug-me types who irritate and bring their insecurities and problems along and dump them out as if that's their famous shrimp fondue and everyone must have a taste. And learning to not only put up with these folks but to love them is one of the things families are for.

It matters so much to me that these people love me back and respect me and support me. When relatives are there for a baptism or a school play or any event that shows their interest in you—boy, that's love. It really feels good to know that you matter to people and that they'll take time to go for a walk or have a long chat with you because you're family. What a solid foundation!

So often we replace these people with our current friends, thinking that our school buddies' opinions matter most and that their affection is more valuable. We make such a big mistake when we do this. Our friends are important, yes, but they are not sealed to us and obligated to stand beside us no matter what happens. They don't feel the same kind of love or loyalty or patience or forgiveness or pride for you as they would if they were your actual brothers and sisters. Family ties can be incredibly strong, and while friendships can be strong and enduring and eternal also, they can't match the potential of the family bonds.

I think about the times we've gone to the temple grounds to see the Christmas lights and, clinging to each other in the chill, we stood and looked at the nativity scene, knowing that each one of us had the same beautiful beliefs and the same love of God. I looked up at the twinkling lights in all the trees, their sparkle blurred by the tears in my eyes. Then I glanced over at Dad. His cheeks were streaked with tears, unashamed. I learned it's okay to cry from my father, not from my friends. I learned the real meaning of Christmas from my family, not from my friends.

Families teach us so many things that friends never can. For one thing, they teach us the practical skills we need in life: how to manage our money, how to be generous, how to build a shed or ride a bike or sail a boat or decorate a room or straighten a closet or scour a sink or weave a rug or clean a fish. Families teach us to control our anger. We are forced to get along with other personalities and make sacrifices; we learn to share. We learn to love even when others hurt us. We can't walk away, and so we learn to forgive and love. We learn loyalty; we defend one of our own when he or she is under attack. We learn to work toward common goals and pray for each other. We learn to take time for little children and old people. We learn to serve others, and we learn that we're pretty wonderful children of God and have the right to high self-esteem.

To me the home is an oasis, a cozy retreat from the storms of "life out there." Outsiders can ridicule or wear me down, but the minute I walk into the house, the familiar picture frames on the piano, the delicate wind chimes outside the patio window, the antique egg timer on the stove, the doilies Grandma tatted, the worn blue slippers Dad left beside his favorite chair, the needlepoint pillow Barb made, the yeasty smell of fresh dough rising in a ceramic bowl, faint traces of Mom's perfume, the smell of the grass outside as Dad mows it, the hum of his mower, the comforting tones of my mom's voice as she soothes some aching heart over the telephone in the bedroom, the silken fluff of Seymour the guard cat who slinks between my legs and rubs his sides against them, the distant echo of kids laughing at the playground down the street—all of it soothes me and massages my soul. I love to come home. I may get yelled at or frustrated here, I may make lots of mistakes here, I may have a lot of work to do here—but there's love in the air, love as thick and delicious as Mom's pumpkin bread. You can love your friends and give to them and learn from them and enjoy them, but you will never have that same "family feeling" with them.

When we're told to "honor our father and mother" it goes beyond obeying them. To me it means, "Do something noble with their name. Live up to all you can be and make them proud of you." To honor someone is much more than to simply obey them or put up with them.

Lots of Church leaders have told us that heaven is an extension of the ideal home. I used to hear that back in the days when Bill and Darin were teasing me to death and I'd think, "What else is there besides heaven, then?" It was as if I were at a travel agency, looking at brochures and saying, "Give me something besides cathedrals and museums, please."

And then I realized that I have to do my part to make the home happy. I had been sitting there waiting for everyone else to make a pleasant environment for me! So I learned that it really takes individual effort in communication—really opening up and really listening as well, serving others in and out of the family, patience, hard work, humor, and enthusiasm. And the biggest discovery I made was that I could influence the harmony in our home if I tried to build up the self-esteem of those around me. A huge bonus caught me by surprise: my own self-esteem grew as a result! Families truly are forever, and their preservation is worth any price we have to pay. We may never mold a perfect family out of the materials we're given. We might struggle and endure for a long time. But along the way, in the effort, we will grow personally and benefit from trying. And anyway, sometimes the differences are what give families their own special style.

I was in the bathroom brushing my teeth the other day, and my dad came in, pretending we were in a TV commercial. (I told you, sometimes my dad can be really corny.) He said, "Aha! Using those extra brighteners for Prince Charming, eh?"

I rolled my eyes and mumbled through the suds. "Oh, Dad, c'mon."

When he knows he's embarrassing me it seems to spur him on to greater heights (or deeper lows, depending on how you look at it).

"Guess there won't be any sparkling fluoride toothpaste left for the rest of the family," he said, his voice melodramatic as he grinned into an imaginary TV camera.

I bent over to spit and then thought, Well, he really is asking for this. So I turned and gave him a big slobbery, foamy kiss on his cheek.

"Aauck! What are you doing?" he hollered, grabbing a towel. His golden TV announcer's tones were buried in terry cloth.

Mother heard his howling and came running. "What happened?" Then she saw Dad wiping the toothpaste off on a clean towel, and she snatched it away from him.

"I just washed that!" she snapped.

Dad looked at her, with toothpaste dripping onto his shirt and said, "Janet, what in the world do you think towels are for?"

"Rinse yourself off, first," Mom said, clutching the towel to her as if it were a delicate baby.

"Oh, I can't believe this," Dad moaned and splashed some water on his cheek.

I was laughing hysterically and rinsed my mouth out.

Mother just shook her head and walked out. "Sometimes I wonder what's wrong with you two. You're both so weird."

Dad dried off his face and hollered down the hall to Mother, "She's the weird one! She wiped toothpaste all over my face! I'm the only sane one in the family. You're saving towels like they're an endangered species, and Louisa's in here putting toothpaste on me! How about endangered fathers?"

"Yep, you're the only sane one here," I said as I walked out. And then to Dad's imaginary film crew, "Cut and print, fellas. I'd say that's a wrap."

MYTH 6

Missionary Work Takes Too Much Time and Trouble

Some time ago we had a Young Women lesson on fellowshipping our school friends. Sister Gillman quoted President John Taylor on missionaries: "Why, says the Lord, with you I will confound the nations of the earth, with you I will overturn their kingdoms."

It was easy to get all charged up (it sounded so easy!) and race off to junior high the next day ready to have a mass student body baptism.

And then reality hit us: Some of these kids aren't interested. Kelly Matheson sat on a bench in the locker room and leaned back against the lockers with a bang. "I can't believe it," she said. "I thought if we just acted really confident, then no matter who we talked to, they'd say, 'Sure, I'll try it.' I've never felt so rejected in my life!"

I was brushing my hair and turned to talk to her. "I know. Everybody I asked just looked at me like, 'What is this—a joke?'" I went over and sat by Kelly, and we brooded through the first few minutes of lunch.

"I can't understand someone not even wanting to know," she said. "I mean, don't they at least wonder where they came from?"

I kicked the toe of my shoe against the bench facing us and let my heel bounce on the cement. "Maybe we're doing something wrong. Let's go talk to Sister Gillman on the way home."

Kelly and I both knew it was the Lord's will to have missionary work. In class we had heard another quote from John Taylor: "Our mission is to preach the Gospel, and then to gather the people who embrace it. And why? That there might be a nucleus formed, a people gathered who would be under the inspiration of the Almighty, and who would be willing to listen to the voice of God, a people who would receive and obey His word when it was made known to them. And this people in their gathered condition are called Zion, or the pure in heart."

So we understood that God isn't satisfied when a handful of people have testimonies; he isn't satisfied to think that we sit at home quietly knowing the truth. He really does want us to share it. Missionary work is not just somebody's hasty notion. So why had we failed? We had tried, hadn't we?

Sister Gillman was our teacher and had challenged us to approach everyone we thought would be receptive and just invite them to a Mutual party. How hard could that be? Trouble was, most kids asked what Mutual was, and when we mentioned church, they could feel the ropes tightening around them. Most of them backed off fast.

Kelly and I rang the doorbell. The Gillman's terrier, Ernestine, came yapping to the door, so I knew Sister Gillman was home. Ernestine is the world's phoniest dog. When the Gillmans are home she practically peels the paint off the door with the steam from her breath. She goes into a wild fit of barking, trying to show off for her owners. You'd think she was a Doberman pinscher. But when they're gone, Ernestine hides under the bed and trembles. Some watchdog.

Sister Gillman pulled the door open. Satisfied that she had sufficiently warned the world of her vicious nature, Ernestine crept back to her green pillow by the fireplace.

We explained our disappointment to Sister Gillman. "You promised," Kelly said, almost blaming her for the day's failure.

Sister Gillman smiled. She has crinkly wrinkles at the edges of her eyes, but they're not unattractive. They somehow make her whole face twinkle with enthusiasm and wisdom.

"Louisa, Kelly," she said, and held one of our hands in each of hers. "I'm so proud of you for doing what you promised." She looked at us both, as if waiting for us to speak, but we had nothing to say.

"Don't you see where you went wrong?" she asked.

I looked at Kelly. Kelly looked back at me. We were both blank, so we looked at Sister Gillman.

"You have to be prayerful. You don't just toss out the Golden Questions like confetti."

I smiled and listened.

"You have to be selective," she said. "You pray about it and make sure you set the right example and be sincere. Really let the kids know you want *them*, especially, to come to the party. Otherwise, it looks like you're out there with a butterfly net just sweeping up anybody who'll slow down enough for you to catch them."

I thought about it. She was right: Kelly and I had been asking kids to the party whom we'd never even spoken to before. No wonder they sensed something wasn't right. They probably felt like we were just inviting them to get points. And I guess we were. We just thought it sounded so easy and would be so fun to get all these kids baptized. But Sister Gillman really had a point. We needed to be a lot more careful, not so reckless.

"That doesn't mean you only pick the pretty ones or the popular ones or the smart ones. It might be the least Mormon-looking person in your class. But it should be someone you feel inspired to ask."

"How do you know when you're inspired?" I asked. And then it hit me. Missionary work isn't easy! It's not as if you can just announce into a crowd, "Hey, I'm a Mormon and if any of you guys are interested, just ask me, okay?" You have to pray about it and set an example and study so you can answer questions and live so that people will want what you have. That means no grumbling, no being miserable, no acting like a jerk. And to know when you're inspired you really have to be living close to the Lord. You truly have to learn about the people you're trying to friendship and take a genuine interest in them. Sister Gillman says you have to love people into the gospel. It takes a lot of time and effort.

When Kelly and I left her house, we had a lot to think about. First of all, we had to be extra nice to the kids we had invited, so that in the future they'd realize our interest was genuine, not just a frivolous "by-the- way." We didn't want to use the confetti approach anymore.

"I don't know," Kelly said. "If you ask me, it's just too hard. I mean, Sister Gillman even said that not everyone is ready to accept the gospel. I don't think *anyone* is at our school. They're all so liberal, into drugs, so immoral. They don't care."

I walked along with her, thinking. "It is a lot harder than I thought," I said. "I mean, you can't just say, 'Here, sign up for your baptism.'"

She laughed. "No way. Can you imagine Freddie Greenblatt as a Mormon?"

We howled. We thought of some other unlikely prospects, too: kids who were so far off the deep end it would take a minor miracle to get them interested.

And we got feeling pretty self-righteous. "I say we just set a good example and wait for them to come to us," Kelly said.

I agreed. Going to trouble was just that—trouble. It took too much time to focus in on somebody and become a close friend and love them and share with them and research all the answers to all their questions. What a pain.

So we "kicked back" and went to the Mutual party alone, no tagalong investigators to worry about.

And then a month or so later when I was praying, I felt an uneasy wave sweep over me, and I opened my eyes. What was that bothering me? It was as though I had a very important thing to say or ask and I couldn't think of what it was and it was bad or scary or something.

I just knelt there in my room for a while, listening with my eyes open and waiting for the idea to surface. I could hear our grandfather clock chiming out in the living room.

My hands felt cold and my forehead was clammy. All over I felt a creepy sensation, as if I were praying a lie or something. I thought back about what I had just said in my prayer. "Please bless the prophet, his counselors, the apostles, the stake president and bishop, and all the missionaries."

On the word *missionaries* I felt that ache in my chest again. A thought popped into my head, just in the form of two words: "Help them."

Huh? Who, me? Help who? The missionaries?

Uh-oh. I think I'm supposed to help the missionaries, and I haven't been doing it.

And then the clammy chill left me, and I felt a warm, glowing goodness all over—from deep within me. It was as though I were suddenly relaxed, yet concentrating very hard. And it occurred to me that I hadn't been doing one single thing to help the missionaries. My prayer was filled with standard Mormon phrases ("all those things we stand in need of . . .") and no commitments on my part. I was asking God to do everything while I coasted along in Lazy Lane.

I prayed again, for the strength and determination I would need to reach out to people who weren't willing to reach back—yet.

When I stood up I felt more relieved than I'd felt in a long time. I'd been honest and told Heavenly Father that missionary work seemed like a bother but that I knew this was the wrong attitude. I asked him to help me *want* to do right.

And he did. It was just after Thanksgiving, and a bunch of us were in the library working on oral reports for history class.

Shelly Wiskett, the only person I know who could get straight A's even if all the classes were in Portuguese or Finnish, was on library aide duty and kept glancing over at our less-than-muffled group. Finally I whispered to Kelly, Heather, and the others to hold it down. "C'mon, we're being too rowdy," I said.

They gradually calmed down, and we immersed ourselves in Patrick Henry and Benjamin Franklin.

When I got up to find a book, Shelly Wiskett followed me. "Thanks for quieting them down," she whispered. "I get into trouble if I let the place get loud."

I smiled and asked her where early American history heroes were.

"They're dead, I think," she said.

And I laughed. She giggled, too, and we quickly hushed ourselves up, peeking between the books to see if anyone had heard us.

And that was the beginning of a wonderful friendship. Shelly told me she really liked history, and then I did what I imagine skydivers do: I held my breath and jumped.

"Have you ever read the Book of Mormon?" I asked. She shook her head. Well, I thought, at least she can't howl right in my face; we're in a library. Then I told her I'd bring her a copy the next day (which meant calling my mom and asking her to find the elders or drive to the temple and buy some copies, which she did with no small amount of difficulty).

Anyway, Shelly read it and cried. She stopped me in the hall and hugged me. I don't know when I had felt so happy. Shelly took the missionary lessons, and her parents let her get baptized within two months. Her brother, Evan, was baptized three months after that.

It was the most amazing, glorious thing. And suddenly I realized that all the "trouble" and "work" of the missionary effort is not trouble or work at all but the most rewarding part. It was so fun to become friends with Shelly. I had always thought she was a brainy snob, but it was only jealousy on my part—and on the part of the other kids— that made me label her that way.

I learned so much just from watching this one friend come into the gospel. I learned that a testimony, like love, is one of the only things that actually increases as you give it away.

Suddenly the sacrament meant more to me, too. You know, when you take the sacrament you are promising to be a representative, a missionary.

I also learned that it gets easier the more you do it. Each time I bring up my religion now, it's easier than the last time. As long as I'm sincere and approaching people with genuine loving interest, the fear evaporates.

I learned also that even if it didn't get easier—if it somehow got harder—it would still be worth it. I guess it's like the way Barbara describes having a baby: No matter how tough it is, the result makes it all worthwhile.

And I learned that youth is the best time—the best. Most kids don't have many of life's answers, and here you are, holding the whole bagful. You stand out, and young people want the serenity and joy that you have. Young kids aren't set in their ways like they might be later. They don't have an objecting spouse. They are seeking truth and identity, and the gospel gives them both.

To be a good missionary you have to be converted yourself. I struggled with that some time ago, and I know it can be a bear. But if you genuinely want a testimony and you'll do what it takes to get one, I know you can have one. I *know* you will. You have to have desire; you have to fast, pray, and listen; you have to study and attend church; and you have to *live* it. Try it on just like test-driving a car. Truly live the gospel for a couple of months, and you won't be able to deny its truthfulness.

Satan doesn't sleep, I guess; and, say what you will about him, you've got to give him credit for persistence. It seems he zooms in on people just after they set a baptism date, and I've watched—and cried— as some of my favorite people have backed down under his pressure and temptation.

He tempts me not to do missionary work, too. This Satan guy gets around. But we just have to plug along and step over him and know that Heavenly Father will help us defeat him.

Missionary work is too important to put off like Kelly and I used to. Kelly's been working on a couple of kids in her music class, and we both have great hopes for them. Kelly says she even wants to go on a mission someday. Her sister laughs, but I'll bet Kelly does it.

That brings me to another point about missionary work: the girl whose boyfriend is on a mission. Kelly has a big sister, Rebecca, who's at BYU and is "waiting" for a missionary. She waits for a missionary like I wait for malaria. If her missionary came home today she would die. This girl "has an understanding" with half the football team, four guys in the law school, and two premeds. "I'm not actually engaged," she says when she comes home. "But we've talked about it."

Good grief—what does she do, discuss engagement as a twentieth-century phenomenon? Half the guys claim to be certain that they knew Rebecca in the pre-existence and that they agreed to meet or marry on earth. Knowing Rebecca, it's entirely possible. Although it sounds like the guys are a couple of berries shy of a bushel themselves. I mean you don't have to be Jewish to look at her situation and see that something here just isn't kosher.

These poor guys that she's leading on—they're probably all just waiting for her to finally sigh and say, "Okay, okay, I'll marry you." Meanwhile, she's writing these "hurry home" letters to Mitch, who's off serving the Lord in some remote region of the Philippines, for crying out loud. Mitch hasn't got a clue as to what Rebecca is doing, and every once in awhile Kelly threatens to write and tell him (usually when Kelly wants something from Rebecca. Needless to say, Kelly always gets it).

I'll tell you, when Mitch finally comes home I would give anything for a front row seat to watch what happens when he sees her bulletin board literally plastered with various young men whose hearts all belong to Rebecca. Wait until he sees the shoebox full of those tiny floral cards that come with a dozen long-stemmed roses. (The love letters outgrew *their* shoebox and now are in a box that a stereo *with speakers* came in.)

I think it's terrible, and I don't know what Rebecca's trying to prove. She's told so many lies she can't even remember which story goes with which boyfriend. How she finds time to study I will never know. Maybe she doesn't. Anyway, Kelly and I are pretty disillusioned with Rebecca. I know I never want to be that dishonest, especially when it can be so hurtful. Poor Mitch. Poor Tom, Dick, and Harry, and everybody else, too.

I've decided that the best thing to tell a guy who's going on a mission is, "I can't promise that I won't date. But right now I'm not interested in getting engaged until you can come home and we can see how things would be between us. You're that important to me."

And if he's not, I think you should just tell him, "Let's just write and keep the friendship growing, and when you get back, we'll take it from there."

That way you've made no promises and told no lies. You should say whatever's really honest. Any guy worth waiting for will respect that and won't try to extract an uncomfortable promise from you. Besides, if you sit home every night while he's away, you might go lurpy on him. You need to keep active friendships and develop yourself in ways outside of letter writing, after all. If, after you've dated enough men to know, you still select your missionary, then he'll know you did some comparison shopping before you bought the best.

Both my brothers went on missions, and they completely agree. Bill had a girl write to him (who, by the way, was Number One in my book, if only because she took over at the chocolate chip cookie controls and gave me a two-year break so that I didn't have to cook them so often). But he said he wishes he hadn't had a girl "waiting" for him. He half expected her to greet him at passenger arrival by tossing a net over him and pulling him in like a snagged porpoise. She really distracted him from the work and kept him thinking about romance too much.

Darin, on the other hand, didn't have a girl friend when he left (still doesn't and never will if he doesn't learn to cook, I tell him), and he said it was much better. He watched other guys live from postal delivery to postal delivery and was glad he didn't have to endure the Dear John letters or the sentimental slurpy stuff in some of their cards. "It was great," Darin says. "They'd get boxes of candy and homemade treats, but we all got to eat it, and only the other guys were still on the hook with some girl." I can just see Darin gobbling up everybody's care packages while the other elders were left to write the thank-you notes and carry on long-distance relationships. But I do think he was smart to go on his mission unattached and able to give his full attention to the work (even if his missionary journal is filled with a few too many critiques on the dinners various members served them).

And I really am proud that both my brothers went on missions. I'm letting every guy I date know—when it comes up—that I absolutely want to marry a returned missionary. Why should I settle for less? I'm willing to do everything I can to improve myself and serve the Lord, and he should be willing to do the same. Who knows—maybe I'll even go on a mission myself. How will I convince my sons someday that they should go on a mission if their dad never found the time?

And then if I date a guy who leaves for a mission and asks me to write, I'm not going to tell him all about my dates and the dances and movies and music and ball games and things that he's missing out on. I'm going to be friendly and fun but keep the letters mainly spiritual and try to encourage him in his work. If missionary work is anything like what I've experienced so far, I know there will be a lot of discouraging times. So I'm going to be optimistic and encouraging, and I'll send inspirational clippings and care packages. But that's it. No passionate prose, no whining for him to hurry home. No telling him how well I remember his wavy hair or his dazzling eyes. No telling him how lonely

I am and then pulling a Rebecca on him and flirting like a cheap idiot. I'll bet you anything when Mitch gets home, he's going to take one look at Rebecca's face, and nobody will have to tell him a word about what she's been up to; Mitch will see it in her eyes.

He'll see that vacant, giddy, glazed expression of hers, which has found its way into too many fellows' hearts. He'll wonder if her testimony is tucked away in her jewelry box behind half a dozen love lockets. He'll probably be gentleman enough to wait until they're alone rather than dump her right there at the airport in front of everybody.

He'll take her for a walk or a drive and he'll make her stop jabbering for a minute and she'll look up at him and he'll say, "Rebecca, I've been gathering the Saints and converting people to the gospel for the last two years. What have you been collecting?"

She'll look stupidly back at him, and he'll ask her how many boyfriends are waiting for her to call them back, and she'll blush. Then Mitch will say, "Rebecca, I knew you were no good from the start. I'm moving on to a *real* woman: Louisa Barker."

Okay, okay, so it's a fantasy. We can all dream, right? Mitch is not only going to be a returned missionary, he's a bright, humble, funny, charming, talented guy. And okay, okay—he's also gorgeous.

Let me tell you about this other really great-looking guy, Brian Westcombe. He's a priest who inadvertently did a big favor for our Sunday School teacher one day by mentioning how silly he thought it was when girls whispered and giggled. You should have heard the absolute silence that reigned in that room forever after. See, although none of us dared admit it to each other, we girls each had a huge crush on Brian, and if he'd said he thought girls with hair looked silly, we'd have gladly gone out and shaved our heads—anything for Brian.

But a couple of months ago he said something in class that really knocked him off his pedestal. Brother Vittorio was giving a lesson on goals and wrote a few on the board, like graduate, get married in the temple, maintain good health, and things like that. And when he wrote "serve a mission" Brian laughed.

"No way. I'm trying out for the majors," Brian said. "My coach and my dad both agree with me, too."

Brian's dad isn't a member, so I wasn't surprised about him. But I was surprised at Brian. I had thought he had a testimony. I mean, it's not like we sit around and share gospel insights over pizza, but I just sort of assumed he believed in the Church and would go on a mission someday.

"What if you don't make the majors?" Brother Vittorio asked.

"Then I'll go into business, and I sure can't afford to take two years off just to poke around some jungle for converts."

Everything was quiet, and we all stared at Brian. He was sitting there, all cocky and proud of his glib reply. A couple of the other guys chuckled then, ashamed to admit they were considering missions, even though I know James Olbern is planning to go, and he was one of the ones who laughed.

I looked down at Brian's shoes. Italian, imported, sexy. Yesterday I would have kissed the ground they walked on. Today I thought of his feet as sweaty jock feet, probably covered with warts and athlete's foot, smelly feet that make you nauseated just to look at them.

Then I looked back at Brian's face, where a disgusting smirk was firmly planted. You are a loser, I thought. You might make the majors, you might be the star pitcher, you might win the World Series and endorse underwear for the rest of your life, but in my book you are a loser. And you know, I never looked at Brian with much respect after that. I still tried to be his friend, but no way did my heart pound when he walked in. Instead I felt sorry for him, sorry for his dad, sorry for his coach, sorry for whatever poor girl he marries someday.

I decided right then that there are plenty of good-looking guys, smart guys, witty guys, well-built guys, tender guys, fun guys—who are willing to go on missions. I don't have to settle for one who won't. And two years— big deal! My dad went on a mission back when they served for two and a half years! And he never regretted a minute of it.

Good luck at the ball game, Brian. You'll need it.

MYTH 7

I'm Grown Up; I Can Make All My Own Decisions

It has finally occurred to me that anyone who *wants* to have that kind of responsibility is not mature enough to have it! After my parents let me dabble a bit in my own decision making, I ended the experiment by concluding that I might be smart in some areas, but in those that take wisdom and experience I'd just as soon rely on my folks and let them have that heavy load.

I'd been complaining that they were controlling my life too much; the reigns were so tight I was choking, I said. Dad rolled his eyes. Mom sighed. I braced myself to hear them say I was going through "the same thing the other kids went through," and sure enough, Dad said, "Well, Janet, it looks like it's time to let her find out about freedom, same as we did for the others."

You know just once I'd like to think I have stepped upon new territory, some new adolescent progress that hasn't been tried in every other home in the country since the day America was founded. Whenever I think I've made a brilliant discovery or suggested a novel plan, I find out every kid who ever passed this way before me thought he had the same solution to teenage oppression and the same unwavering confidence that he, too, would be different.

It's as if the parents of America are sitting on the curb while we insist upon parading our problems before them, and we're sure that this time they'll slap their cheeks and say, "My gosh—our kid is right! She *is* the first truly mature teenager! Look at that ingenious presentation!"

Instead, they watch us prance by, almost yawning with boredom at the repetition of it all. ("Oh—*another* marching band?")

"Okay, okay, do your worst," I said, shifting my weight and getting ready for their challenge. Dad smiled and asked me to sit down.

"In what areas would.you like to make more of your own decisions?" he asked.

"In *every* area! I'm old enough to know what's best for me in everything."

"Okay," he said.

My jaw dropped into my lap. "You mean it?"

So for the next two weeks I got to eat all the junk food I wanted, I didn't have to do any homework, I stayed up late and watched all the old movies I could, I stayed on the telephone for hours, I skipped church, I slept late, and I left clothes and shoes all over my bedroom.

I nearly died.

For one thing, I got sicker than a dog due to my lack of sleep and my diet of sweets and deep-fried foods. My eyes were sore and bleary, my friends were tired of talking to me, I missed getting to go to a couple of church parties because I wasn't there to hear about them, I got way behind in seminary and schoolwork—I mean *severely* behind and I blew a couple of tests—and lost my chance to be in the regional scripture chase and also to compete in the science fair. My clothes were never clean or pressed when I needed them, and I spent hours just looking for lost shoes and belts.

Worst of all, my spiritual battery wound down. I became negative, sassy, depressed, and grouchy without the inspiration I used to get at church. Creepy thoughts crept into the spaces that used to be filled with religion. It was awful.

At the end of two weeks, on antibiotics and megavitamins, I practically crawled to the dinner table and begged for some decent food.

Mom's mouth twisted and her nostrils flared as she tried to squelch a grin. "Vegetables?" she squeaked, trying not to laugh out loud and say, "I told you so, I told you so! Hee-hee!"

I nodded and climbed onto my chair. About half way through the meal Dad and Mom began exchanging glances and nods, and I could sense that the experiment was over.

"So how's it been going the last two weeks?" Dad asked. I looked over at him, bleary eyed. "Oh, I don't know," I said. Ha—I knew, all right. It had been like a roller coaster ride that lasts for thirty years. It seems fun at first, but after awhile you think you'd rather jump than go around once more.

He smiled. "Still think you're mature enough to make all your own decisions?"

I nodded. "I just made the wrong ones this time, that's all," I said. "When the newness wears off I'll be fine."

He laughed, and Mom joined him. "I'll tell you what *I* learned," he said. "I learned that you're a typical seventeen-year-old, even if you like to think you're all grown up."

I scowled. Nobody likes to be told they're anything less than brilliant, at least not in my family. We all like to harbor secret suspicions that we're adopted and in reality carry the genes of Nobel Prize winners, prophets, statesmen, and angels. And maybe even a movie star or sports figure. To face the fact that you are just like everybody else in a lot of ways is not easy.

"A really mature person would have gone right along doing what they knew to be right," Mom said. "You'd have kept your room straight for one thing. You'd have gone to seminary."

I moaned. A temperature of 103 degrees, a plummeting grade point average, eyes that look like scrambled eggs, and now complaints from my very own mother on top of it.

Dad laughed. "I think she's suffered enough, Janet."

I nodded. "I should have waited a couple of months to try the experiment," I said. "In two months I'll be ready. Two months, easy."

Dad grinned. "That's what Harold Weisbaum said."

"Who's Harold Weisbaum?" Mom and I asked simultaneously.

"He was an athlete I used to know who said he could get ready for the Olympics in two months." Dad sipped his orange juice.

"I never heard of him," I said.

Dad stood and patted my shoulder. "That's why."

Ugh. I hate to play right into his hands like that. I groaned and ate some wholesome food for a change, then slithered back to my bed like a snake on his last vertebrae. Mom came in a little later with a snake tray. I mean a snack tray.

"I must confess that the last two weeks taught me what a gift you have for the dramatic," she said. "I think you might have gotten sick anyway, Louisa."

I sniffed. "Yeah, maybe my resistance was already down. But what terrible timing."

"You did pretty well, actually," she said. "I mean, you didn't get arrested or run away from home or take drugs or date a motorcycle rider."

I smiled. My mom thinks the worst fate that can ever befall a girl is to date a motorcycle rider. I try to point out to her that plenty of conservative businessmen, with coattails flapping, drive to work on fuel-efficient motorcycles and that hard-working, ambitious students often drive to hard college classes on similar machines and that even our honorable police force has one or two, but my mom is oblivious to such examples. In her mind everyone who gets onto a motorcycle is a Hell's Angel, headed for a tattoo shop to add another snarling spider to his shoulder. They're all heroin addicts who have fried their brains until the engine noise no longer bothers them. They're con artists with quick getaway machines who lure young lovelies onto the backs of their bikes—and away from a mother's protection— only to turn them into greasy, tough Motorcycle Mamas who disgrace the family name forever.

Bill called that evening, and somehow, I found the strength to dash for the phone in my usual style. I told him about the horrendous two weeks my parents had just forced me to have.

He laughed. "You did a lot better than I did," he said. "I crashed a speedboat, got suspended from school, got hauled in to talk to the bishop— you got off easy!"

My eyes popped. This is Bill? The family nerd who never even made a chancy chess move? Bill, who took Marianne Parker out for eight months before he even gave her a good night kiss? Bill, whose grade school teachers all kissed him good-bye every day? I was stunned.

"Yeah, well, the bigger they are the harder they fall," I said. He laughed. It was nice to know I wasn't the only seventeen-year-old in history to blow it.

Since then I have learned a thing or two about maturity. I have a little way to go before I arrive (a much smaller way, I tell my folks, than *they* think it is), but at least I'm on my way.

I know that before we're really grown up and able to decide most things on our own, we have to acknowledge that God knows more than we do. We should remember to consult him when we make decisions. I hadn't done this even once during my "trial run." I had assumed that he was only to be asked on the major decisions later in life, about whom to marry and whether to move to Kansas. It suddenly hit me: If I don't ask for his guidance on the small things now, how will I recognize his input later on the big things?

I think of the scripture that says "Choose you this day whom ye will serve . . ." (Joshua 24:15) and how important it is for us to choose to serve the Lord, not seeking after material things or base pleasures. I guess most of us in the Church think of that scripture as telling us to serve the Lord and not Satan.

But something else popped out of that scripture for me: the words "this day." That means we shouldn't just defer this choice until after the party this weekend. In fact, you can't "decide to decide later" anyway! We make our choice every day, whether we like it or not. Our decision *is* made, and it shows in everything we do. Don't just choose to serve the Lord, choose to do it *today.*

I believe in memorizing hymns and then singing them softly inside our heads when we're in moments of temptation or weakness. They keep us strong, and I know it works. Anyway, the one that has lately been on my mind goes, "Do what is right; let the consequence follow; Battle for freedom in spirit and might; And with stout hearts look ye forth till tomorrow; God will protect you; then do what is right!" It's all about a trait that mature people have: courage.

Courage is so hard to have, but without it we're at the mercy of everyone we meet. We'll bow and bend to please others, never standing up for what we know is true. We have to have courage to make wise, ethical choices and to return to Heavenly Father. We have to have courage to be good parents someday. We have to have courage if we want to keep our virtue in this sexually permissive time. Courage will save our necks—really! It's an essential trait, not an optional one.

We have to do as the hymn says and let the consequence follow, knowing that God will protect us. If we really do what we know is right, we shouldn't worry about the consequences; we should feel serene and calm, knowing that God will bless us for staying true. And think of your future children (I do this a lot—only I picture them looking like a cross between me and Robert Redford). But seriously, you want your kids to be proud of you and to know that you were strong when you were young—stronger than the other kids.

Humility is another element of maturity. Now you know that there's the wrong kind of pride and the good kind of pride, right? It's wrong to be arrogantly proud of your new boat, but it's right to be proud of your kid when he learns to share his toys, okay? Well humility is the opposite of the wrong kind of pride.

People who have poor self-opinions and who continually criticize themselves are not humble, as is often thought. They're not truly humble in the sense that Christ asked us to be. In fact, they are denigrating a creation of God and impairing their personal growth—two things he would not condone. True humility comes after a person has healthy self-esteem.

When we see braggarts and overly proud snobs, we should know that this simply indicates poor self-opinion again. They suffer from the same problems as the gloomy self-belittlers. It's just another symptom of the same disease.

Only when you really know you have value and that God loves you, can you gratefully reflect upon the blessings of God's love and know that you feel neither the need to puff yourself up nor to put yourself down. You don't have to present "an image." Then you can feel really humble, knowing how great God is and how great is your own potential.

When you're humble there's no need to bluster or assert. You don't have to be the smart aleck, the tough guy, the "sweet lil' ol' dummy me" type, the bossy type. You just have a calm sense of peace, and you don't overreact. When someone is rude to you, you don't have to jump into the arena and get even. When someone compliments you, you don't have to squirm and deny it. In both cases you just see the whole picture and see the incident in the eternal scheme of things and smile. There's a serenity to humility.

Humility helps us learn lessons from our successes. Humility reminds us that when we excel, we give God the credit. There's no such thing as a great man or a great woman who wasn't also humble. Those whose accomplishments and traits speak for themselves don't have to run around making a big scene over it. They would look like fools and blowhards. Their words would belie their accomplishments, you know?

I think about confidence and humility when I think about Camilla Kimball, the wife of President Spencer W. Kimball. My mom told me that one day she was in Salt Lake City at a ZCMI store, not long after it had opened. Sister Kimball was standing a little distance away but was turning and looking about, obviously a bit lost. At last she asked a salesclerk where the escalator was, and Mom saw the salesclerk roll her eyes and impatiently snap, "Over there—over there!"

Mom had half a mind to go and knock the salesclerk silly and ask her if she had any idea who this elderly lady was, but Sister Kimball immediately set the proper example for her and she bit her tongue.

Sister Kimball just looked lovingly back at this young idiot (my words, not anybody else's) and thanked her for the direction. Then with perfect dignity and grace, she glided away. Sister Kimball has patience, love, humility, and confidence. She doesn't need to chew everybody out, even when they're rude to her first. She doesn't have to assert or demand or holler back. She just goes on her way, radiating serenity and peace. Wow, to be like that!

I think about serenity as it relates to sports cars. (My mom would say that it is amazing how many things I can think of that relate to sports cars.) Now I will admit that I like sports cars and that maybe I will have to answer for this unnatural craving someday. But I see a sleek, Italian, racy car, and I melt. I'll admit it's awful, and I really must overcome it. But at least I've learned something from it.

I went out with a guy because he drove one of these, okay? It was a rotten and insincere move on my part, and I hope—I think—I have learned my lesson. Anyway, he let me drive it (oh, heaven!) and I made a shocking discovery.

When I pulled up to the intersection and the light went green, everybody else zoomed out ahead, trying to be first off the line—Pintos, Toyotas, Cougars. I just sat back and slowly rolled forward. And I thought to myself, "I have absolutely nothing to prove to these people. I'm sitting here in control of more horsepower than they will ever dream of, and I don't have to screech out ahead to prove I'm fast. I know I'm fast. Ahhh . . ."

And I imagine that's how it feels whenever you're so accomplished or so secure in some field that you don't have to toot your horn anymore.

Another element of maturity is responsibility. I'm not crazy about that word; it always seems to crop up when Mom is standing in the laundry room telling me about the buttons on the washing machine and how to presoak and sort and spin dry. Somehow that word *responsibility* seems to end sentences that start, "Louisa, this is your . . ."

But when you get right down to it, we all have duties and obligations, and if we can't accept them or rise to them, we'll be social misfits forever.

One responsibility we have is to decide what we want in life and not put it off. I know a lot of girls who just don't want to think about it yet. They want to get a tan and go shopping and get ready for a date and read pulp fiction. But plan for the future? No, no thanks.

Yet everything we do is taking us in some direction. Not setting your life's goals and yet living every day is like not looking at a map, yet driving sixty miles an hour down the road. You're going *somewhere* whether you chart a course or not. As long as you're going, why not pick where?

In case that sounds like too much work, I've made the decision for you. Or, rather, you can choose the same stuff I chose. I simply decided that I want the best. I mean it! *I want the best*. The best husband, the best marriage, the best family atmosphere, the best relationship with Jesus—*the best*. I'm not saying the best clothes, the best silverware, the best stereo speakers. I'm talking about high quality spiritual choices. If I want the best marriage I'm going to have to work my tail off, but what I'm saying is that I'm not going to settle for average or adequate. I want, where I can, to make a real difference in my life-style. I want to be the best mom, the best student, the best *me* that I can be. Now maybe you're gifted in some area I'm not, and you'll be a better student, let's say. But if I do my very best, then I'm the best I can be, right? I mean, it's obvious.

And we owe ourselves no less. I've watched people get complacent and settle because they were too lazy to shoot for the moon, and it's sad. I'll never give up trying to be my best, and I don't want you to either.

Okay, to have all these "bests" we have to get out a piece of paper and a pen that writes (a real trick in my house) and write down on the left what we want, then draw a column line and on the right side write the cost of each item. Be brutal and be realistic.

If you write "I want to be a concert musician," then next to that you write how many hours a day you must invest practicing. If you write "I want straight A's," then on the right you write what that will take. If you put down "I want to marry a returned missionary who respects his priesthood and can take me to the temple," then on the right you have to acknowledge that a neat guy like that is going to be looking for a number of things you'd better be willing to bring to the marriage: virtue, cleanliness, intelligence, etc., etc., and maybe it will cost you a little popularity among some of the rowdier kids. Write down whatever it costs. "I want to work for a year before I go to college" might just cost you your whole college experience! "I want a car" might cost you some lazy summer play days as you work to earn the money. "I want six kids" might cost you a career.

Now look over your list, and ask yourself if the price is too high. If being a virgin when you get married is one goal, and if it costs the companionship of a few guys, on my list that's okay. It's priceless, right? That means any price you have to pay to keep it is worth it.

But let's say you have "I want to sail around the world" on your list. And it will cost you your attendance in church for several months, and you're borderline active as it is. Maybe that is too high a price to pay: maybe it would cost you your testimony.

Sometimes our goals and their prices look good, but it's hard to decide to pay the price. Let's say you have "graduate with honors" written down. That's a good goal, but for most people it will take a lot of studying, and you like to play too much. This is when we have to pray for the strength to stay true to our ideals. This is when we have to do some real soul- searching and make commitments and set smaller goals that can get us there one step at a time.

And maybe we set our goals too high sometimes. Maybe a poor student who wants to graduate with honors but is also required to support a crippled parent and seven dependent siblings is really asking too much of herself. Maybe she should be content to be a really terrific person and not give herself ulcers trying to be the Superwoman in every area.

One of my goals was "get along with my parents better," and the price was a lot of personality improvement on my part. I had to stop arguing, start communicating and listening better, stop agreeing with some of my friends who said my folks were old-fashioned, stop trying to take the easy way out of my household chores.

I looked at that goal and the friends that it cost me and I want to tell you, it wasn't an easy decision. "Maybe I'll just stick it out for a few years until I'm away at college or married," I thought. But then I remembered that families are forever and I want to have a close, loving relationship not only in the next life but when I have my own kids and when I'm growing older. So I bit the bullet and determined to give what I had to.

If we decide to go for it, we must pray for the power to resist Satan and for the determination to follow our map.

My two-week experiment taught me a lot about the wisdom that comes with age. A really mature person doesn't deliberately make the wrong choices or frivolous decisions, thinking that tomorrow never comes. I was pretty short- sighted and eager to break all bonds of restriction when my two weeks began. At the end, I was dying for some rules that would make me happy again. A mature person realizes that what she does today will matter in the future, so she proceeds with care and caution rather than in a hasty, reckless manner.

Impatience is a big hallmark of youth, I guess. We can never seem to wait for anything. When we're standing on a corner waiting for our mom to pick us up after baseball practice and she's ten minutes late, we get in the car and tell her we've been waiting for half an hour. When somebody says they heard something about us and they'll tell us later, we grab them by the neck and demand to be told right away. Suspense kills us.

It's worse in little kids. A two-year-old cannot wait five minutes while you scoop the ice cream. He wants it yesterday. And I guess this ability to "defer gratification," as psychologists say, gets more realistic as we age. So being patient and being able to wait things out without falling apart is another good thing to work on if we want to mature.

I think something else about maturity is knowing that we never completely arrive. We never know everything, we are never totally grown up. Even after we die, we continue to progress.

But as we grow, let's hope we learn and gain wisdom. The more mature we can act, the more responsibilities and freedoms we'll get from our parents. Fences and limits and rules exist because we have not yet proven that we know how to govern ourselves.

I hope you'll believe me. I'm just telling you what I've learned near the end of my teens. There is much more to discover (at least there had better be; I need a lot more materials to help me before I charge out into the world in what amounts to my underwear), and this advice is based on a very short life.

But maybe you'll take my word on a point or two and not have to learn the hard way. Duc de La Rochefoucauld, whose name alone makes you slow down and think, also said something that made me pause. He said, "We may give advice, but we do not inspire conduct." And maybe you'll be hardheaded like me and ignore all this, only to come back to it in a couple of years and say, "Oh, yeah. She was right. Sure wish I had listened."

Listen now. Save yourself the two-week trial run.

MYTH 8

Good Grades Are
for Nerds

Boy, I sure learned this one in the nick of time. Three years ago Michelle's brother, Terry, graduated from high school and decided he wanted to go to a big university and he couldn't, because he hadn't taken the right classes in high school. And even in the classes he had taken, his grades were just okay. Terry was a quarterback and vice-president of the class, but when high school was over it didn't count for much.

I remember I was in the ninth grade, and it shook me up to think that already the classes I take and the study habits I develop will determine where I'll be in five years. And where I'll go to college and what kind of work I'll be able to do. It really opened my eyes.

Some of the girls in my Mutual class aren't that worried about college. They figure they'll get married to some great guy with a great future and he'll provide some great income and they can sit back and grind wheat in their spare time.

But our bishop came in and talked to us and told us all to prepare for not one, but two or three careers. He said it isn't that we'll all become corporate giants or career girls, but he said times have changed and young couples often need a second income, just to buy a house. And anyway, your husband could die or become disabled, or you may not even marry—and you have to be able to support yourself. Plus, after your kids are grown (Mom, are you listening?) then you can dip back into your profession and enjoy working and growing in your career again.

I haven't decided what I want to do (*not* build airplanes, I think—news that will probably be a big relief to the aircraft industry), but I'm going to take the harder solids and study and get good grades so that whatever I decide later on, I'll be prepared.

Plus, I've decided it's only the jerks who tease you if you get good grades, anyway. They're jealous and five years after high school, they'll still be nowhere. They won't have any goals or plans and they'll just drift away and live off the government or something.

Whenever I've gotten a really great report card it's felt good. I know I've earned those high marks, and I like knowing I'm above average. In citizenship, too.

I saw a bumper sticker the other day that said, "If you think education is expensive, you should try ignorance." You know, that's absolutely true. So many kids think college is either too expensive or too time consuming. Yet if they don't go, they forfeit the chance to earn as much money, and they miss out on the rewarding experience of a well-rounded education.

My folks took me on a trip once—on a steamship from Seattle to Victoria, British Columbia. It was a fantastic trip, and I loved everything I saw and did. But of all the experiences we had, the one that most impressed me was one we had on board the ship.

We had lots of time to see the boat and chat with other passengers. I sat a few feet away from a group of people who, from snatches of conversation I could hear, were just meeting for the first time. One woman impressed me in particular.

She was not a beautiful woman, but she was well groomed and looked like she had good taste. She wasn't flamboyant, but she sparkled. Why? As I watched her and listened to their conversation, I was fascinated by her wide range of knowledge. One fellow was a petroleum engineer. She asked him all kinds of questions about Saudi Arabia, South Africans who turn coal into gasoline, the price of a barrel, geothermal energy—and all as though they'd been friends forever. She wasn't showing off her knowledge; it just shined naturally. She was so attentive and responsive to what he said that you'd have thought there wasn't another person on the whole ship. Then when someone in the group mentioned an art exhibit, suddenly she knew all about that artist and his training and his influence on the impressionists during his last years. A woman in the group was a magazine editor. I listened in amazement as this brilliant lady began to converse just as easily about advertising, deadlines, and page layouts. On and on it went, and this woman delicately juggled about eight different subjects—always letting the other person feel they were the smartest, yet interjecting just the right comments and questions to keep the ball rolling. People hung on her every word and laughed at her jokes. She was completely enchanting and had that entire group in the palm of her hand! I sat there, wide-eyed and awestruck, wondering if I could ever be so comfortable with such a wide range of people. I wished that one day I could seem so eloquent, so refined, so cultured.

Near the end of the trip I saw her alone at the snack bar getting a sandwich, and I got up the courage to go stand beside her. Maybe some of her class would rub off on me!

To my surprise, she turned and said hello as if she were genuinely interested in me. She hadn't looked especially pretty when I had first glanced at her, but now she seemed beautiful. I said hi back, and she smiled. "I noticed you sitting at the tables earlier. Is this your first time on a ship?"

She had noticed me! On top of seeming to give her full attention to her admirers, she had actually been observing the people in the background.

I told her it was my first time but that I hoped to take similar trips again someday. She made me feel so at ease. We chatted about boats (she knew, of course, where all the fun boat trips were—cruises down the Mississippi, leisurely jaunts to Mexico, even hair-raising raft rides down the Colorado rapids), and finally I took a big breath and said, "How is it you seem to know so much about—so much?"

She smiled again. "Thank you. I suppose I enjoy talking with people and reading. But mostly I tried to study as many different things in college as I could. I still take classes and plan to go to school for the rest of my life."

And that's when I finally saw the difference: Some people go to school to get out. They want a degree so they can get a job, and they take what they "have to" to meet the requirements. *Other* people, like this woman, consider schooling a marvelous opportunity to become well educated. They are fine tuning their minds and really using what they learn. It's not something they dread and lumber through like an unwilling elephant; they sprint. They soak up all they can because they love it, and then it radiates from them and makes them fascinating.

That is the difference between "going to school" and "getting an education." I want to be like that woman, caught up in the world of thought, able to express myself and ask questions confidently, of anybody I meet.

And the Church teaches that idea, too. Our early Church leaders put education high on their list of priorities. In the Doctrine and Covenants it says, "It is impossible for a man to be saved in ignorance"

(D&C 131:6) and "if a person gains more knowledge and intelligence in this life through his diligence and obedience than another, he will have so much the advantage in the world to come" (D&C 130:19).

A lot of our sayings about education originated with Joseph Smith. For example, he said, "The glory of God is intelligence" (D&C 93:36), "Seek learning, even by study and also by faith" (D&C 88:118), and "Whatever principle of intelligence we attain unto in this life, it will rise with us in the resurrection" (D&C 130:18).

Beyond personal satisfaction, education has a lot of practical benefits. I'm not saying you *must* have degrees to get certain jobs— we can all find some tycoon who dropped out of second grade—but I do know there's a direct correlation, nowadays especially, between how well we do in school and how high we rise in the job market. If we graduate with average grades, we can't pick and choose our colleges. If we barely squeak through college, we might not get admitted into graduate school. If we don't go to graduate school, (in some cases) we might not be able to get that plum job we want. And why not? Because somebody else who was willing to study and sacrifice will leap ahead of us and snatch it. Why shouldn't an employer hire the best applicant?

I get pretty good grades, and I want to tell you how to do it. First of all, decide that you want them. Have a strong desire and realize that if you get good grades now, you can keep up that momentum and it will be easier to get good grades later.

Develop good study habits. Do homework as it's assigned, and get it out of the way. Don't wait until the last minute to write up that report.

Take good notes and, as you write things down, organize it in your head. Not every teacher teaches things in an orderly fashion, but most do, and if you write things down this way you'll save a lot of study time.

Get into a good study group, not a bunch of kids who goof off but ones who can test you and explain things for you.

When you study for a test, make up test questions for yourself. You will be truly amazed—I mean this—when you take the test and see that your teacher came up with so many of the identical questions you did.

Be an extramiler. Don't just do the minimum that's required. If you have to use three sources for a report, use five. If your teacher likes artwork, really put time into making yours stand out.

Learn how to think. Now that might sound silly at first, but do you have any idea how many people wade all the way through school and still can't think straight? (Drive on any Los Angeles freeway, and your estimate of this number will go up.)

I mean it; people follow orders like little combat robots who do as they're told, and some of these folks get pretty decent grades. But too few people ever really think or question or analyze the information they're being fed. They just take notes and then spit it all back out onto their test papers.

A good way to learn how to think is to engage in conversations that make you stretch. Talk to adults, talk to educators, talk to college kids, talk to the brainy bunch at school. Engage in debates—even join the debate team. This will teach you to organize your thoughts, almost as if you have a filing card box in your head. In fact, you have a better deal than that: You have a human mind, which tops any computer in the world. Use it. Don't be timid about engaging in a conversation with experts; the smartest people around are the ones who aren't afraid to ask "dumb questions."

I've lately been trying to date super smart guys, too. And I've found out they're a lot more fun; they have really witty minds and sharp senses of humor. I went out with a guy to a Church Christmas party once. His name was Milton, and I almost didn't go because I thought he had weird hair. But my mom, who's desperately afraid I'll marry out of the Church, said, "Go ahead and go. Maybe Milton won't be the man you marry, but maybe you'll meet someone there who will be." Good old Mom—planning my wedding well in advance.

So I went. And do you know what? I had an absolutely fabulous time. Milton has since moved to Utah, but if he were here I would definitely be flirting my head off, trying to get him to take me out again.

The party was in the cultural hall and started with the choir director handing out sheet music to everyone for a sing-along. "If this is Handel's *Messiah* I might as well tell you now that I have to be home by eleven," Milton whispered.

I laughed, and two old ladies in front of me turned around. I cleared my throat and winked at Milton. The sheet music came down the aisle, and we each took one.

"What self-respecting American doesn't know the lyrics to 'Jingle Bells'?" Milton asked, his low voice in my ear. I laughed again.

Then before we began singing, Sister Thurmann announced that she would be playing a piece on the piano that was a lullaby which was sung to babies at the time of Christ. "Just think," she said, her voice gripped with emotion, "Mary sang this exact same song to baby Jesus."

I smiled. How nice, I thought. What a treat. I looked around at other happy faces there, people anxious to hear a song that Jesus himself heard.

And then Milton whispered to me, "Right. They found cassette tapes along with the Dead Sea Scrolls in the caves at Qumran."

And then I lost it. I was laughing so hard I had to get up and go out into the parking lot to hold my sides and recover. Milton left with me, whispering all the way, "Am I the only person in the whole Church who can see the impossibility of this?"

I wiped tears of laughter from my eyes. "I can't believe you said that."

"Well, think about it," Milton argued, his happy eyes twinkling. "We barely have the Bible, for heaven's sake. How on earth do they think a lullaby was recorded and preserved all these years? They didn't even have eight-note octaves in those days—or pianos."

I finally stopped wheezing and caught my breath. Then I looked at Milton with his innocent yet comical expression, and I burst out laughing again. Faint strains of a thoroughly modern-sounding song were filtering out into the night air.

"Why do we buy into everything we hear?" he whispered. "Doesn't anybody ever stop and say, 'Now wait a minute; that's not possible'?"

Now Milton laughed and told me my mascara was dripping onto my blouse. I dabbed it off and my giggling finally died down. I thought about what he said and how truly right he was. We hear so-called inspirational stories or rumors sometimes, and we never stop to think that maybe it's all fluff, designed to tug at our emotions and elicit a big, dramatic response. But the gospel is so beautiful and so exciting without all that hype; it's a shame there's still so much of it to sift out.

Milton and I went back in, and he promised to save all his insights until after the program so I wouldn't have to dart from my chair in further hysterics. But we had such a wonderful time, and I thought to myself, "No wonder he gets straight A's. He's a genius; he sees right through everything to the very core, and he has a clever way of turning what he hears into something entertaining."

Oh, Milton, please move back.

Anyway, I think I was telling you the importance of learning how to think, to listen critically, to question and to ponder.

Next, tell your teachers, individually, that you consider yourself a good student and you want to do well in that class. Ask if there are extracredit assignments you can do. Don't be shy about asking for tutoring if you fall behind. If a teacher knows that you are a conscientious student who really wants to excel, she'll bend over backwards trying to help you. It's a turn-on to teachers to find that one of their students is enthusiastic about learning their subject.

Remember that teachers talk to each other. If you're a troublemaker in biology, chances are your teacher will complain about you in the faculty lounge, and your reputation will spill over into driver's ed and choir as well. It works to your advantage, too: If you make the class a joy to teach, instructors will rave about you to their colleagues, and others will expect you to shine in their classes also.

Sit on the first or second row. Studies have shown that the closer you sit to the instructor, the higher your grades will be. You miss less of the lecture, you're less inclined to be distracted by other students, and you tend to participate in class more.

Always be prepared with pens and paper.

When you know you have to be absent, ask the teacher ahead of time what assignments and reading you can do; that way you won't get behind.

Read the newspaper every day and stay current. Know what's being thought and said and discovered in the world.

I was talking about grades with Michelle the other day.

Hers are average, and she really wants to improve them. We decided her basic problem isn't that she can't learn the material; it's that she's unorganized. She needs a regular time to study, a set routine. She needs to take organized notes and really listen attentively when she's in class. (This is easy to do; you're there anyway, right?)

At first when I suggested some of these things she whined that it all took too much time. Then I laughed. "Michelle," I said, "How much free time do I have, and how much do you have?"

"Oh, you have a lot more free time than I do," she said. "Tons more."

I smiled. "That is exactly right. When you take organized notes, when you do your studying as soon as you get home, you aren't more restricted; you're free! You give yourself loads of time to play and goof around." It's like having an organized closet (Mom would love to hear me say this). If you put your shoes away and in order, then you never waste time scrambling all over the house in a daily hunt for your shoes. You go to the closet and bingo—there they are. You put them on, and you don't have to spend another minute thinking about lost shoes. Those who are afraid of such "restriction" are actually imposing constraints upon themselves by having to devote five minutes a day to a shoe safari. It's so simple, yet I must have a dozen friends who can't understand this.

Improve your reading skills. Become not only a rapid reader but a thorough one, even if you have to take a summer school class in this to accomplish it. It will pay off over and over and save you all kinds of time.

You may ask how I know all this. Easy. I asked my teachers what makes a good student. And you know what? After I asked, they all began to look at me a new way, as if I'd now identified myself as an achiever, a good kid, a person who studies. They all like me better than before because they know I'm not just in school to "get out." I'm here to learn something.

It all comes down to attitude. Just like the lady on the boat ride. If you're really charged up about a certain subject, you dive in and go the extra mile anyway. It's no longer a chore but a thrill. When you really enjoy a subject, you do better in it. And the better you do, the more you enjoy it. The whole experience becomes a cycle of achievement and growth.

As long as you're learning, your mind stays active and you never seem "old." The joy of learning is something we all deserve, something we all need to live happy lives, and something we can all give to ourselves. We don't need anybody else to hand it to us.

For a teenager who likes her independence, I'd say that's a pretty good place to start.

MYTH 9

It's Okay to Taste Alcohol or Try Smoking

Shanna Luben was gorgeous. She was not only gorgeous, she was classy. Plenty of girls have pretty features, but Shanna had flair and elegance that set her light-years ahead of the pack. When Shanna had to make a dress in home ec, she didn't use a pattern. Instead, she tore a designer's sketch out of the newspaper, added a few embellishments of her own, ripped up some fabric, sewed it together, and knocked the socks off of everybody at the school fashion show. She was breathtaking.

When a bunch of kids held a stupid demonstration in the counseling office—trying to get out of ever needing hall passes—and Principal Hubert turned purple and threatened to kick them all out of school forevermore (which he legally couldn't do, but he lost his cool), Shanna was the one who saved the day. Someone had called the newspapers, and a TV film crew was even headed for the school to cover this so-called news event, but by the time they got there everything had blown over and the kids were back in class and Principal Hubert was cracking jokes with the reporters. Somehow Shanna had walked into the chaos in the counseling office and, as usual, all fell silent in her beautiful presence. She looked at the angry faces and standoff positions of administrators versus students and smiled. Then she asked each side to calmly explain their side of the issue. She asked questions that made everybody think, and she suggested a compromise. Who knows, maybe everyone was swept away by her regal charm; she reminded me of Grace Kelly, and maybe others had the same reaction. Anyway, whatever she said, they all agreed and shook hands and resumed their normal activities. Shanna just smiled and floated away, like the Good Fairy who has kissed your forehead and is now on her way to restore peace in some other remote region of the universe.

Whenever you wanted to know the best way to behave in a certain situation or what the eloquent, diplomatic thing to say might be or how to dress just perfectly for an occasion, Shanna was the standard. You knew you were safe if you did "whatever Shanna Luben would do." She was not just a girl who looked and walked like a film goddess. She had warmth and kindness and humor; she got stared at by men and women alike, whenever she went anywhere or said anything.

So why was Shanna Luben dead on arrival at McCarthy General Hospital from an overdose of speed? Why did a beautiful girl with everything going for her—everything!—have to trash her life and die that way?

At school we held a special memorial, and Shanna's family said they would like to have some doctors and drug abuse experts be part of the program. The school said it could be an important teaching opportunity to prevent the same thing from happening to other students. They said it would be an awakening experience for us.

Let me tell you, it was.

The first doctor to speak said that it's easier for young people to become addicted because they go into it so much more innocently than adults do. They think they can just experiment and quit when they want to. They often don't realize how serious the substances are. Sometimes they think they're just joining in and doing what everybody else is doing.

Adults act this way, too, but more of them understand the seriousness of their experimentation. They know more medical information, and they've seen friends go through addictions and dry-outs—whether from smoking, alcohol, or whatever.

So despite the fact that we think we know a lot about drugs, we don't. Even medical science discovers new things all the time.

A young person who plays with cigarettes, alcohol, and other drugs is in a worse position than somebody who takes up these habits when they're, say, thirty. For one thing, tissues are still developing in a young person, and you thwart their natural growth. Then you add all those extra years to the amount of time that you will be using drugs, and by the time you're forty, you'll look sixty.

The first doctor ended his speech by saying that every year they find more problems caused by cigarettes and alcohol. "Don't ever start," he said. "Just don't take that first step."

Shanna's mom got up and, controlling her tears as best she could, told how Shanna had begun with iced tea. Iced tea! Then, since the caffeine in it would give her a boost of energy, she began drinking coffee to stay awake while she studied. When coffee began staining Shanna's teeth, she switched to speed.

Shanna's mom stopped speaking, then spoke again with a broken voice. She said she had allowed Shanna to take the pills under the guise that they were for dieting. Shanna had done some modeling and wanted to stay trim. Her mother figured there was no harm in it.

Little did she know that Shanna was getting so wound up she needed downers to help her relax. Shanna was on a roller coaster ride that she couldn't control. It went faster and faster until it finally jumped the tracks and plunged to the ground below.

We sat in the audience, nearly every one of us with tear-streaked faces, listening to the story of Shanna's addiction. Any suicide is tragic, but for some reason Shanna's hit us all pretty hard. Maybe it was because she had so much to live for and had the unequaled respect of everyone who knew her. We hadn't just known her; we had aspired to be like her. None of us had any idea that her happy life could turn into such a pit of turmoil.

After it happened, of course, you could look back at the change in her behavior during the last year. She had pulled away from her friends, her appearance had degenerated, and we had all tried not to believe the rumors we'd heard.

The next doctor who spoke said that education is vital. He said ignorance was a poor excuse, and we all ought to feel motivated to learn all we can about the dangers of these things so that we can better resist temptation when it arises.

He told us that smoking not only causes the lung cancer and heart disease we all know about; it causes lung damage to every smoker. Every one. "Every smoker will have damage," he said, "period. Without any question. I'm talking about bronchitis. emphysema, asthma, pulmonary failure which can lead to death, damaged blood vessels, heart attacks, strokes with paralysis, ulcers, loss of legs due to circulation diseases, loss of skin's elastic tissue (early aging and wrinkles!), senility from poor circulation to the brain, 'dog breath,' yellow fingers and stained teeth. People who think they can smoke and escape all these problems are not living in reality," he said.

Then he talked about alcohol and said it causes a lot of similar disorders, especially problems for blood vessels. "Alcohol impairs circulation to the heart and brain. It causes strokes and heart attacks. It inflicts direct toxic damage to the liver. Make no mistake: Alcohol is a poison.

It causes ulcers, gastritis (inflammation of the stomach), aging of the skin including permanent red 'spider veins,' and brain damage." He said alcohol actually shrinks the brain and causes loss of intelligence, which is another name for stupidity. "The more you drink the stupider you get," he said. And it also hurts the nerves that control your muscles. It can weaken your muscles and even cause burning pains and paralysis in the legs.

Then he talked about tea and coffee and how foolish people are when they don't realize these are harmful drugs. A cup of coffee contains 150 miligrams of caffeine, which artificially stimulates the heart and kidneys. It even causes cancer of the colon.

Finally Shanna's father spoke and, with tears rolling down his cheeks, begged us to stay away from anything that could cause addiction. His talk was short but powerful. It left every one of us choked up. He ended it by just saying, "Please. Please."

That night when I wrote in my journal I mentioned how firmly I am convinced that the Church is true. Medical science has finally corroborated what Joseph Smith revealed more than 150 years ago! Almost point by point, we're seeing the scientists recommend the same identical things that the Lord outlined for us over a century ago. We've been told to eat meat sparingly, and look at what they're telling us about cholesterol now. A high-fat diet is terrible! We were told to eat grains and fruits in their season, and sure enough, that's one of the most healthful things you can do. We were told to get rest; look at Shanna trying to get by with less.

The whole Word of Wisdom is about moderation, and look at the tremendously life-threatening problems people cause when they go to extremes. I think about the anorexic/bulemic girls I know (you'd be surprised how many there are) and how opposite this is from what the Word of Wisdom tells us. I notice a number of these girls in the Church, and they usually come from conservative families where considerable emphasis is placed upon looks and appearance. It has broken up otherwise wonderful families, and a friend of Heather's had a brother who finally had to divorce his wife because of this destructive behavior. He just couldn't cope with it any longer; she'd gorge and stuff herself, then throw it all up. He said it was worse than living with an alcoholic.

I remember as a kid listening to our stake president, who was also a doctor. He said that obesity is a major problem and that it indicates an inability to live the Word of Wisdom. He stressed to the youth that we maintain a sensibly slender weight. He said that if you're fat as a teenager you'll have a much harder time losing weight as an adult. (He said "almost impossible—maybe 1 percent can do it.") He said the key to dieting is attitude. "Don't dart from one wacky diet to the next. Realize that you have to modify your life-style permanently. Snack on celery and carrots instead of junk food. Be active in sports, and keep your level of exercise high." It's all such common sense!

When I go to a party and they're serving liquor, my parents have asked me to call them and they'll come get me. I know it sounds old-fashioned to a lot of kids, but I find nothing fun in watching a bunch of kids get loud and pushy and nauseated. I like to be around people who are emotionally relaxed enough so that they can be funny and enjoyable without any outside help. I'm not particularly impressed with girls who get themselves drunk so they can have sex and then deny any knowledge of it the following day. And I don't find a loud, belligerent, foul-mouthed guy with a belly full of beer very appealing. Who would? When I go to a party and the drugs or booze start flowing, I'm not the least bit embarrassed to go to the phone and ask my folks to get me out of there. I'd rather watch the world's oldest rerun on TV than sit and watch my friends waste their brains away.

And I can't believe how many teenage alcoholics there are! I thought the choicest (and, okay, brightest) spirits were being sent to earth in the latter days; so why are there so many acting so stupid? At school there's a guy in the tenth grade whose parents both died last year from alcohol- related problems. And they were young parents still in their thirties. The father died of a completely shot liver and pancreas, and the mother mixed some kind of prescription with her daily dinner wine. Now this poor guy has no parents! What a tragedy. He said they had both been heavy drinkers in their teens, and already they had been paying for it with early health problems.

My mom helped me research alcoholism for a report in my health class and she showed me a copy of a talk by Elder Hartman Rector, Jr. He quoted Harvard University nutritionist Dr. Jean Mayer as saying, "Every year we convert in this nation into alcoholic liquor enough grain to feed 50 million people in the starving nations."

Imagine! I think of all the people whining and crying about world hunger and overpopulation. Then I look at what is spent on alcohol, cigarettes, cocaine and other hard drugs—even on such frivolous things as cosmetics and even my beloved records. It makes you stop and think. If we really wanted to help the starving masses, we could sure cut out a lot of nonessential products.

Elder Rector went on, "In the United States there are 95 million drinkers, of whom 10 million are confirmed alcoholics. These 10 million alcoholics in the United States cost this nation $10 billion a year counted in lost time, slow downs in work, illnesses, mistakes resulting in spoiled materials, domestic problems, and the rest of the attendant evils that go with alcoholism.

"Also, it has been proven that alcoholism shortens the life of every alcoholic from 10 to 12 years: 250,000 new alcoholics are added to this total every year. The Connecticut state mental health commissioner reports that 40 percent of the cases in the state mental health hospitals are attributed directly to alcohol. Superior Judge John A. Starbaro of Chicago has said that '75 percent of all the divorce cases I have heard resulted from alcohol.' Alcohol is responsible for one-half of the total traffic deaths in the United States. There are 25,000 persons killed every year on the highways in the U.S. It might be interesting to note that we had 57,000 American servicemen killed in the Vietnam War. This total is nearly duplicated every two years on America's highways."

And Elder Rector said all that back in 1975. Can you imagine how much worse the statistics are today with our increased population?

I liked what Elder Theodore M. Burton said once: "If a warning label such as is found on every package of cigarettes were placed on every can or package of dog or cat food, the purchase and use of such pet foods would come to a screeching halt. People would never even think of feeding such material to their pets. People think too much of their dog or cat to so carelessly endanger its life. Yet they ignore those very same warnings when they are given to human beings. One must draw the conclusion that people have a higher regard for their pets than they have for themselves or for their own children. It is a sobering thought."

At Harvard University, President Charles W. Eliot gave a talk and said to the students, "My dear freshmen, I want you to remember that tobacco in any form destroys the brain, and you have none to spare."

You know, the trouble with all this information is that information isn't enough. Someone who's weak enough to buckle under a little peer pressure isn't going to become a wall of strength and determination just because she reads a few statistics.

What it really takes to keep the Word of Wisdom is a strong testimony and a real love of God and self. When we genuinely like who we are and what we believe in, we don't have to go along with any crowd but the crowd we lead. We feel comfortable speaking up and saying we don't drink or take drugs. You wouldn't eat food you don't like, even if everyone else was doing it, would you?

Imagine: You hate liver, but you go to a party where all the kids are nibbling on liver instead of potato chips. You wouldn't do it just to be part of the crowd, right? You might even laugh and say, "No way, not even if you paid me!" Why can't we feel the same way about coffee, tea, and alcohol? In fact, I'd rather have liver! At least it's good for you.

One way to begin to have strength is to imagine that your bishop or that the prophet is with you. Don't indulge in anything they'd disapprove of.

A good standard is to avoid anything—even people or jokes or books or fashions or teachers or music—that dulls your senses or pulls you from God. Now of course not every friend you have is going to be perfect and make you want to fall to your knees in gratitude or burst into song with joy. But you know the difference between people who basically uplift you and inspire you, and people who seem to bring out your negative traits. And let's face it; we all have a dark side that we try to overcome. Most of us struggle against laziness and selfishness and lots of other negative qualities. Some people help us on that upward climb, and some people only make us feel worse about life and about ourselves.

Using substances which alter our moods or our health can only bring us misery. Even what seems to be temporary happiness or momentary acceptance at school isn't even that. From the kids I've talked to, I've learned that even being high doesn't erase problems. They're still there, and you know it. Then you come back to reality, and they're bigger than ever. There's just no winning when you cheat at the health game.

I think about Shanna sometimes and how painful her life must have been towards the end. She must have felt absolutely enslaved to her habits, as if she had given her soul away. And I suppose she had.

I remember her dad, how utterly devastated he looked in the auditorium that day. I will never forget his earnest plea when he looked down into our wet faces and simply said, "Please. Please."

MYTH 10

Life's Goodies Are for Everyone Else

I wonder if I've stumbled onto a buried treasure sometimes. I feel like I kicked my toe against the dirt in the backyard, and up gushed an oil geyser. Or as if I opened my closet door one morning and, instead of hangers and clothes, I looked out into a sparkling landscape of lush trees, fragrant blossoms, natural fountains, and singing birds.

Somehow I've discovered a paradise that is hidden from the general public: I've learned that I can have all the happiness that is possible!

Now you may not think this is any big deal, but believe me, a great majority of my friends somehow think they don't *deserve* the best, and it keeps them from ever reaching out for it. The world seems full of people who are unconsciously trying to fail: people who settle for abusive boyfriends, people who settle for poor grades, people who never try to join anything or run for anything because they're sure they wouldn't make it. It's incredible!

During one family home evening, I mentioned this to my folks, and we talked about how sad it is that so few people realize their fantastic potential. So many of my friends think life is just a treadmill: You drag yourself through high school, get a job you'll probably hate, enter into a difficult marriage, take on the tedious task of raising children, then die a long-awaited and very exhausting death.

So few people ever get excited about life and go after all the goodies. Somewhere along the line they get the idea that all the joys and pleasures of living are for other people who have better luck. They don't realize that Heavenly Father wants every single one of us to have joy.

I have an aunt named Luna (Dad says everybody was waiting for her to marry some guy with the last name of Tick, but this never happened), and she is her own biggest stumbling block.

Aunt Luna looks at the dark side of everything. If the sun shines she says it's scorching the ground. If it rains she calls the weather dismal. If the wind blows she whines about all the dirt in the air. And whenever something nice is about to happen to her, she takes a negative outlook and almost makes things go wrong.

When we went up into the canyon for a picnic, she kept frowning up at the sky and telling us it would rain for sure. When we were finally gathering up our ice chest and packing things to go home after a gloriously sunny day, I said, "Well, Aunt Luna, it didn't rain after all!"

She just huffed and got into the car. "Did too. It rained ants."

No one has ever seen Aunt Luna laugh or even look neutral. I feel so sorry for her. She can't accept a compliment or see herself as someone who can be happy. Somewhere she got the notion that happiness is for others. Her lot in life is to be a workhorse.

I'm not knocking work. I think it's great to develop a love of achievement and an enjoyment of a job well done. But Aunt Luna's theory is that work is life and anyone who stops to take a rest or wipe his brow is lazy. She never allows herself a holiday and never uses her good china or her lacy nightgowns. She always buys the cheapest cuts of meat and never indulges in dessert. She sets her alarm to get up at 6:00 a.m., even on her birthday, and doesn't own a television.

Aunt Luna, I might add, is rich. Not just "doing well" or "living comfortably." Aunt Luna's husband made a killing in real estate and left her a bundle. I mean, we're talking a million. But does Aunt Luna use it to bless her own life as well as the lives of her family members? No. It sits in the bank because Aunt Luna doesn't feel deserving of an occasional movie or new dress. She scrimps along and cooks hamburger on a skillet with a broken handle and keeps an egg timer by her phone so she won't run up a big bill.

Aunt Luna is not stingy or mean. She loves her family and is very loyal to every one of them. I wouldn't doubt it if she revised her will every time a distant cousin's baby was born. She always remembers everyone's birthday (with a phone call after the rates go down). So she's good-hearted. Her problem is that she doesn't believe she deserves to be happy. She has tons of valuable land and could sell it tomorrow to people who are continually phoning her with offers. But she won't take a cruise or go out to dinner or even think about owning more than three pairs of shoes.

Aunt Luna's trouble is that Aunt Luna doesn't like Aunt Luna. If she did, she'd allow herself an occasional pampering, whatever that happened to entail. She'd enjoy life and have a happy outlook. Her eyebrows would relax, and all the kinks would melt out.

And I see a lot of my friends who are headed for the same unhappy future that Aunt Luna has. They won't speak to the cute guy in geometry because "Oh, he'd never be interested in me, anyway." They don't try to work up enthusiasm for losing weight because "I just come from a fat family, anyway." They don't try to do well in school because "Nobody in our family is very studious or smart." They don't speak up in class because "I always say the wrong thing," and they don't extend themselves to have fun at a party because "Nobody ever likes me anyhow."

They have no idea that the whole world is just lying there in front of them, waiting to be their red carpet. Somewhere they got the idea that they must settle for mediocre and that they don't deserve to grasp the top rung of the happiness ladder.

Sometimes they think it's sinful or extravagant to enjoy life. Like my Aunt Luna—when a vase breaks she glues it back together instead of buying a new one. It's thrifty and practical and stays clear of false pride, so I can see her reasoning. It's just that she's forcing herself into this dreary life of cultural starvation. I'll bet she hasn't had a good belly laugh in twenty years. Even when we visit and somebody makes a joke, she bunches her lips up and tries not to crack a smile.

One time a cousin of mine asked her why she didn't just set aside a few minutes each day for play. Aunt Luna looked at her as if she had suggested robbing a bank

"Certainly not," Aunt Luna sniffed. "Life's too short to be light-minded."

Later in the kitchen, my cousin said, "Life's too short not to spend *some* time having fun," and I agreed.

Aunt Luna thinks that there are two states of being: sinners who laugh and fritter their time away, and hard workers who clomp along in their murky bog awaiting a martyr's reward after death.

But look at Joseph Smith! He was known to be loads of fun, and he really set an ideal example of perfect balance in life: He was incredibly spiritual, but he was also a great self-taught intellectual and he knew the value of recreation. I would love to have known him, if only for his sense of humor.

My cousin is the opposite of Aunt Luna. Her name is Sauna (if you thought Louisa May Alcott Ziona was bad). Imagine naming a sweet little baby *Sauna*! Her mother says she liked the sound of it, and it never occurred to her that her daughter would get called Steambath and Hot Tub all her life.

"Why didn't you just name her Shauna?" she was asked once. Sauna's mother shrugged. "Sounds like someone's trying to say *Sauna* with a lisp," she said.

Okay, the whole world is wrong, and Sauna's mom is right. If you knew Sauna, you wouldn't care what her name was: Everybody loves her. She's always full of pep and vigor, always willing to laugh and have a good time. Yet she's an accomplished violinist and an excellent seamstress, so you know she doesn't just play and waste time. She loves life and has an exuberant approach to it. She knows we're here to have struggles and to achieve difficult goals, but she knows how to intersperse a little "down time" to rejuvenate and renew. Sauna really likes herself. She gave me a quote by President Harold B. Lee once that said, "I recall the prayer of the old English weaver, '0 God, help me to hold a high opinion of myself.' That should be the prayer of every soul; not an abnormally developed self-esteem that becomes haughtiness, conceit, or arrogance, but a righteous self-respect that might be defined as 'belief in one's own worth, worth to God, and worth to man.'"

When we believe that we are inherently good and lovable, then we are even better able to love others. It feels so good to be kind and do favors for other people. When we genuinely like ourselves, we allow ourselves to have that delicious feeling which comes through service.

To really believe that we deserve a happy life, sometimes we have to finish our parents' work for them. I truly think most parents do the very best they know how and that most kids don't show enough appreciation for this (myself included, I try to admit more often than just on Mother's Day).

But despite their good intentions, I think a lot of parents simply don't realize how to give a kid self-esteem. They raise kids the way they were raised for the most part, and who knows whether that was right? Still, they try and shouldn't be blamed when they are so sincere.

So maybe you come from a good family where an honest effort was made, but—TA DA!—there you are without enough self-esteem anyhow.

Instead of blaming our parents or our environment or our looks or our poverty or whatever scapegoat people use, we should just say, "Okay. Here's the raw material: me. Now it's up to me to take it and fashion something super from it." After all, Heavenly Father put the seeds of godhood into all of us; we can advance toward that of our own will if we want to.

We can actually finish the job of parenting for ourselves. This means erasing all those "you're no good" messages that some of us get growing up. Maybe no one ever said that to you in so many words. But somehow, through watching others accept failure or through being told to be content with misery, some of us get the idea that we should never strive for anything better. We must believe that we can have it and that we deserve it.

President Kimball once said, "God is your father. He loves you. He and your mother in heaven value you beyond any measure. They gave your eternal intelligence spirit form, just as your earthly mother and father have given you a mortal body. You are unique. One of a kind, made of the eternal intelligence which gives you claim upon eternal life.

"Let there be no question in your mind about your value as an individual. The whole intent of the gospel plan is to provide an opportunity for each of you to reach your fullest potential, which is eternal progression and the possibility of godhood."

In seminary about a year ago, there was a girl named Jeannie. She was living with a family in another ward for that school year, and though none of us knew the exact details, we got the impression that Jeannie came from a bad home setting and had been abused by her father and neglected by her mother.

We all felt sorry for her and tried to become friends. We invited her to go along to the movies; we even planned a special party just so we could ask her to come to it. I called her up one day and asked if she'd like to go shopping. Kelly invited her to go to Palm Springs for a whole weekend. The seminary teacher had invited Jeannie to dinner numerous times.

But always the answer was no. I couldn't understand it; we genuinely wanted to help her and be friends with her. Even if I hadn't known about her background, I would have wanted to get to know her; she was cute and funny and seemed to be an interesting girl.

And then one day in seminary I figured out why she never let us do anything for her. Brother Scott was talking about the three degrees of glory and said, "Who in here would like to go to the celestial kingdom?" Of course we all chuckled and raised our hands—why not want the top?

But Jeannie didn't raise hers. Brother Scott said, "Jeannie, don't you want to go to the celestial kingdom?"

"Oh, sure, but there's no way," she said.

"What do you mean?" Brother Scott asked.

"Well, maybe you could make it, but no way could I ever go there," Jeannie said. "That's for Church leaders and stuff."

Brother Scott looked as if he wanted to cry for her; he honestly felt so bad that she had given up hope.

I stared at my notebook so none of the other kids could see the tears welling up in my own eyes: Jeannie thinks she's a nobody. She thinks she can never have the ultimate happiness.

After class Brother Scott talked to her, and the next day he gave a whole lecture on the fact that every single one of us can—and should—aim for the celestial kingdom. Heavenly Father wants all of us to go there.

At school I looked for Jeannie and finally found her in the gym. She was shooting baskets and was darn good at it.

"How 'bout some one-on-one?" I said. This was a hilarious remark to fall from my lips, as I've never played one-on-one in my life. I'm really short and not very fast, and the only reason I know what one-on-one is, is because I've watched my friends' brothers play it.

"Oh, no thanks. I was just messin' around," Jeannie said.

Whew! I tried not to show my relief. (I knew she'd cream me, and I wasn't up to it that day; I had just bombed a biology test.) But I did say, "Well, looks like I'd be in over my head, anyway. You're really good. Are you going to try out for the team?"

Jeannie laughed sarcastically. "Yeah, right."

I was surprised. "Why not?"

"I'm sure."

I sat down on a bench and watched her. I'm no expert, but if I were a guy I would think twice about challenging her to a game that meant a lot to me to win.

"Jeannie, you are really fantastic. You could make it easy," I said. "Look at that!"

She sunk a difficult shot and dribbled the ball down to the other basket.

"Louisa, thanks for trying to boost me up or whatever it is you're doing. But I've been around. I know my status."

Whoa. I sat there, stunned. All this time Jeannie had been thinking that we were just "being nice," that we were just inviting her over and talking to her because we got some kind of credit in heaven or in Mutual or something.

"Boost you up, huh?" I said. "You think we're all a bunch of phonies, huh? Just because we feel sorry for you, huh?" I was really getting mad about it. I don't like being accused of fakery or insincerity.

"Well, yeah, now that you put it that way. You guys already have your friends. I'm different."

"Oh yeah?" I was taking off my sweater now and kicking off my shoes. "Throw me that ball."

I ran out on the court and caught the basketball. I remember thinking, "Boy, these balls are hard. And big." I probably didn't dribble right and I might have looked ridiculous, but Jeannie didn't laugh. She just put her hands on her knees, concentrated, and we played. Hard.

If Mitch or Chuck or any other gorgeous hunk had walked in right then— or even if Freddie Greenblatt had run behind me snorting—I wouldn't have noticed. I was concentrating as hard as I ever have. I was furious with Jeannie, and I wanted to beat her. If she wanted to be lousy at basketball, I was going to make it all come true for her. I was going to show her that I don't put up with rejection. I was sick of trying to be her friend—and I mean really trying—only to have her accuse me of phoniness.

She snatched the ball from me as I was bouncing it and dribbled circles around me. She threw the ball, and it hit the backboard. I caught it as it bounced off—what is that, a rebound?—then I zoomed behind her to try for a basket.

I jumped as high as I ever have in my life and threw the ball at the hoop. I missed. For the first time in my life I saw how hard it is for athletes not to cuss. I really wanted to win!

But I caught the ball again and tried once more. Jeannie got the rebound this time, thundered up to the hoop, and sunk the ball. I pounced on it and flew around the court. This time I actually made a basket! I was exhilarated!

On and on we played, Jeannie getting stronger and more accurate, while I was getting weaker and more frustrated with missing so many shots. I felt like there was a Plexiglas cover over the hoop. I just knew the ball should go through, and then it wouldn't.

But I played until I was nearly exhausted. I wasn't even keeping score, just trying to show her up.

Finally Jeannie sunk another one and turned and said, "That's twenty-one. You want to quit?"

I stood there in the center of the court, panting and sweating like a horse. My knees were trembling, and I knew my muscles would be in knots tomorrow. I could hardly see straight.

"No way," I said, setting my jaw and wiping my hands on my pants. "Let's play all the way to a hundred. I'm just getting warmed up."

She stood there for a minute, and then she laughed. I must have looked a sight with my hair all wet on my forehead and my shirt sticking to my back. One of my toes was poking through my stocking.

I stood there, still panting and gulping while Jeannie, who looked as cool as a milk shake, just laughed at me.

"You are the worst basketball player I have ever seen," she said, sitting down on the bench to catch her breath from laughing.

I looked at her and tried to calm my pounding heart. I knew if I didn't sit down too, I'd probably collapse.

When I sat down, Jeannie slapped me on the knee. "You really are the pits, Louisa." She was still laughing.

And then I started to giggle, too. Thinking back, I could only remember two times that the ball went in. But I threw it a lot.

Coach Randall walked in with a box of baseball gloves (mitts?) and saw us sitting on the bench laughing like a couple of hyenas.

"You girls okay?"

Jeannie nodded. "Just fine, coach."

He did a double take when he saw my red face and hammered outfit. "Louisa, is that you? Are you all right?" He stopped in his tracks.

"Yeah. I was just trying to beat Jeannie, here, at basketball."

"Stick to science, Louisa." Then he disappeared into the locker room.

I leaned back, exhausted. "Well, you beat me fair and square," I said.

Jeannie laughed again. "Louisa, I creamed you. You are truly the worst."

We laughed some more; she was absolutely right. Then Jeannie stopped laughing and looked straight at me. "Louisa, thanks."

"Thanks for what? For being so lousy?"

This time Jeannie didn't laugh. "You may be lousy at playing ball, but you are good at really caring. I'm sorry I didn't believe you."

I smiled. "Sorry I got mad about it."

Jeannie and I stood up and headed for the showers. She seemed softer, less defensive now. She finally believed that I wanted to be her friend.

"I haven't been very friendly I guess," she said.

"Yeah, well, hey. I can take it," I said, pretending to be a tough guy and using my Brooklyn accent.

She laughed again. "Can we be friends?"

"As long as I don't have to play basketball with you," I said. "That's going too far."

We giggled and stood under the soothing hot showers until we felt—at least until I felt—like I could walk home again. Then Jeannie came home from school with me, and she had dinner with us.

Being her friend was hard; she had a lot of defenses and was reluctant to be vulnerable. She had a bad temper and she was moody, but then after what she'd been through, I could understand it. Even so, it was worth it to reach out to her. She was a great girl and loyal to the end. She finally moved back East to live with another relative, but we write occasionally and I'm hoping to see her on a vacation this summer.

The best thing that happened during the year I knew Jeannie, though, was after we had a long talk one evening. She had confided some mistakes she'd made and told me that this is why she never believed she could go to the celestial kingdom: She didn't feel God could ever forgive her.

That night we prayed together. It was an earnest prayer of great intensity, and Jeannie demonstrated a lot more faith than I would have expected; something told me she had prayed a lot during the troubled past she'd had.

We asked Heavenly Father to help Jeannie seek repentance and to give her the courage to see her bishop. She resolved that night to get her life in order. At last Jeannie believed that life's goodies—and the goodies in the next life—could really be hers.

People who think they can never repent or that they can never get organized or that they'll never amount to anything or that their life is a throwaway—are fulfilling old messages that they don't have to! No matter what negative ideas have crept into our feelings about who we are, we must give them up and learn that Heavenly Father wants us all to have the peace and happiness he has. He wants us to enjoy living and to have self-confidence. He wants us to choose good companions and good words. He wants us to surround ourselves, not just with light and happy things but things which keep us on a steady course, things which motivate us and inspire us to do good.

He wants us to develop our talents and to give service to others. If you want to raise your level of self-esteem, try doing good deeds for others. You'll feel great about yourself! You'll know you have value and that you can make a difference to someone.

We have to believe in ourselves. We have to know that we can reach even the highest goals. How else do you think Jeannie finally made the team?

MYTH 11

If It Isn't Easy, Forget It

I walked over to Heather's house not long ago. It's quite a long walk for a city kid, but my mom was raving about the gorgeous weather and she said the lilacs were in full bloom at the McMansion. So, being the sucker that I am for the heady fragrance of a blossom-laden lilac bush, I set out.

The McMansion, by the way, is really just the largest house in the neighborhood and still a far cry from a French chateau or an Italian villa. It's simply a big house where a family named McMurphy lives. Their kids are fairly popular, and we refer to everything they have as McCars, McClothes, McToys. They have a McDog named McWebster and McBird named McElvis. The McMurphy kids play it up and call their parents McMom and McDad (who in turn tell their kids to clean up the McMesses in their McRooms).

Anyway, it's a very unusual family (you probably noticed), but their landscaping is wonderful. Their house is surrounded by beautiful flowers and by what seem to be tropical ferns that belong in a rain forest, and yet here they are, thriving and swaying in the desert breeze at the McMansion.

Mrs. McMurphy says she won't grow any flower that doesn't have a strong fragrance, and as you walk up to their door you are nearly knocked over by the intoxicating whiffs of gardenias, hyacinths, roses, and freesias, depending on what time of year it is. You almost feel like Dorothy in the poppy fields on her way to Emerald City. I think this attention to the nose is a fine idea for Mrs. McMurphy, but I would miss the camellias and irises, myself. So what if a couple of plants have no scent? For the beauty of a ruffled iris it's worth it.

Anyway, I wound around by the McMurphy's and found that the lilacs in front of their house were just in buds and that to get around to the bushes in back you had to fight through a whole jungle of other stuff they haven't trimmed yet (branches and twigs that are undoubtedly the latest development in retirement living for black widow spiders and such). Plus you had to climb over a big pile of sand that the littlest McChild had left some toy dump trucks on. Too much trouble. The McMurphys have so many kids that they don't care if you wander around their place; but it was such an obstacle course that I decided to go on toward Heather's house instead of stopping.

At Heather's I hollered through the screen door and heard her mom shout around the corner of the house to grab some gardening gloves and come on out back. They were all out in their garden pulling weeds.

"Aha! So you're the family making the rest of us look bad with our crummy little dried up gardens," I said. It was true; Heather's family had a spectacular garden filled with glossy, green leaves and bright, plump vegetables.

Ours looked like the stubble you see after a forest fire. It isn't that we didn't try. It's that maybe we didn't try hard enough. We went to stake conference and got all inspired to finally follow the prophet's counsel, and we dashed home and broke up the dirt clods in our "garden area," mixed in some sand and fertilizer (guess who got that job), threw some seeds into the ground, planted some stakes, strung some wire for the beans, watered it, and waited.

Nothing happened. It reminded me of the time in fourth grade when Miss Schuman had us all plant lima beans in little Styrofoam cups, and mine never came up. "Louisa's was infertile," she announced jubilantly to the class, delighted at having a handy example for purposes of instruction. I sat there ashamed and mortified. There is nothing worse than being told you're infertile in the fourth grade.

Dad was not to be discouraged. He went out and bought a special tiller and some chicken wire. Mom sent away for some prehistoric looking vegetable seeds that promised to grow bell peppers the size of a Ford Mustang. Then Dad sent a soil sample to a laboratory.

Finally some pale, spikey sprouts started to poke up through the clay. The next day they bent over and disintegrated.

Then Dad put up a sturdy fence. He bought a special spray gun of insecticide and wrapped black plastic under the tomato bushes (which he finally purchased half-grown).

He bought some white plastic, cone-shaped tents to cover the tops of the tomato plants, but they looked exactly like little miniature Ku Klux Klan hoods, standing all in a row as if at military attention, and

Dad took so much ribbing from the neighbors that he finally pulled the hoods off and just left the black plastic underneath.

Mom sewed a scarecrow, I donated a still pretty respectable pair of Calvin Klein jeans and the name Mortimer, and Dad bought a little lumber for Mortimer to rest upon.

Finally one of the tomato plants looked as if it might surpass the former record of six inches (held briefly by a daring but doomed little sprout which looked suspiciously like a thistle to me), and a little knob on it even looked as though it might someday become an actual tomato. No news from the cabbages or cucumbers.

We watered and waited. Nothing happened. So next, Dad imported some night crawlers. ("I can't believe what you have to pay for one lousy worm," I griped. "Look what we've had to pay for our city councilman," Dad said. He had a point.) Then he found someone who'd sell him some praying mantis insects to eat the pests. "Pray for tomatoes," I whispered to one of them.

Finally the big day came, and Dad led us triumphantly to the garden to pick The Tomato. We stood in breathless anticipation as he twisted it from its home and held it up against the blue sky. It was the size of a golf ball and the color of a carrot.

Carefully, we transported it to the kitchen and Mom, as if performing delicate surgery, sliced slowly through its shiny skin. She handed a tiny piece to Dad and one to me. We tasted it.

"Oh, delicious," I said. I had planned to say this no matter how it tasted because it is not my policy to break my dad's heart after he has waged a literal war against the elements just to produce this one tomato.

"My piece is tart," he said, wrinkling his nose. I looked at my shoes, afraid to let our eyes meet. Mom tasted it. "Well, dear, it's only the first one," she said, trying to buoy enthusiasm. "Maybe it's like a first pancake and you shouldn't eat it."

Dad stared at the mutilated tomato on the counter, its slimy seeds a squishy mockery of his manly strength, his devotion and effort.

"There are not going to be any more tomatoes," he announced, "because there's not going to be any more garden." Then he went into his den to pout. Of course, he would never have admitted that's what he was doing, but Mom and I knew and simply looked at each other.

"He doesn't mean it; he just feels bad," she said. "He'll work on the garden again."

"I know," I said.

But he didn't. The few sprigs of anything that sprouted just died in the ground, and we were left to drive by Heather's house and sigh, wishing we knew her family's secret.

I bent down and started helping them weed. "Your dad ever start another garden?" Heather asked. I shook my head. "He decided that 356 dollars a pound is just too much to pay for tomatoes."

Her parents laughed. Heather's dad pointed over to the side of his garden. "What he needs are some decoy zucchinis."

I looked over at the zucchini plants near the gate, and Heather's dad explained. "I plant these at the entrance so the deer and rabbits will feed on those and leave my good stuff alone. We still get plenty of zucchini. That way everything else is left to grow."

I laughed. "How do you train the animals to come in through the front entrance?" Our critters always descended like a cloud of locusts, coming in from all directions and devouring our plants the way Pac Man gobbles up dots.

"We'll have a garden next spring. You'll see," I said. Of course, the squirrels will probably hold their annual Squirrel Corn-bowling Olympics and Squash Tournament there, as usual. They've already printed the flyers with a map and everything. Mortimer is the key landmark to watch for.

But I had to admire Heather's dad. Trust her family to come up with a creative solution to a problem. They really know how to look on the bright side and use ingenuity to hurdle obstacles. I've noticed Heather's family often takes this approach.

One time I was helping them get ready for a ward dinner, and Heather's mom put on some majestic music, the kind you hear when the knights in shining armor finally return to the castle for their reward from the king. Heather and I laughed. We'd been complaining about how hard it is to make pies from scratch, but when her mom put on the Dvorak record and announced that this was music to make pie crust by, we could only plunge in and let the music lead us triumphantly along. She made the job really fun. (And I have since decided that Wagner is music to grind wheat by, which is to say that I still find it a tough, sweaty job.)

Sister Flynn, our new Laurel teacher, has that same attitude, that same creative outlook to finishing tasks. When an elderly widow in the ward, Sister Coburn, died, we all went over to her home to clean it up for sale; this was our Mutual service project. When we walked in, it was so filthy it literally took your breath away. I've never seen—or even imagined—a less sanitary home. We all tried to conceal our tremendous shock.

Even Sister Flynn looked pretty astonished. The toilet had been broken for a long time, and the carpet in the bathroom was soaked and mildewed. There were piles of newspapers and rubbish in nearly every corner. The walls were covered with grime, and the kitchen counters were splattered with crusty food and dried gravy. Sister Flynn stood there for a while, then turned slowly around. I could see she was wondering where to start.

"What this place needs is a catfish like they have in aquariums," I said. "It could just clamp onto the wall and inch along and eat all the garbage."

The girls laughed, and Sister Flynn smiled. Then her eyes lit up. "Hey— that's it! We'll all be like catfish!"

We stared at her, horrified. But then she explained that instead of trying to tackle the whole house in one afternoon, we could each take a small section at a time and get it to sparkle before attacking the entire place.

It worked beautifully. She even divided up the kitchen counter into eight tiles each. We each took a rag and had fun comparing who could go fastest and who found a good method for really getting the grit off the woodwork. Once she took the job apart and made it a series of smaller jobs, we zoomed through the place. All it took was a new outlook.

And no, it wasn't easy. But it was "do-able," as Sister Flynn would say. It was a good feeling to work and scrub and see the shining results. What a great sense of satisfaction. And after, while we were enjoying our well-deserved root beer floats, I thought about how much I had learned. Originally I had muttered, "If it isn't easy, forget it." But now that I'd been through a tough job like that, I could see what a person would miss if they always had a lazy attitude.

I guess what a lot of us lack is self-discipline. I remember once hearing that David O. McKay suggested doing something difficult each day, in order to be happy. It sounded ironic at first, and I imagined myself doing the dishes or ironing in order to feel happy. Bleah! But I've learned that my attitude of taking it easy didn't make me happy; it just made me lazy and miserable whenever I had work to do—which is almost always. When we force ourselves to do something unpleasant, yet which we need to do, we develop discipline and talents we never knew we had. We become less selfish and more loving toward others.

One of the hardest things for some of my friends is to get organized. Boy, talk about "if it isn't easy, forget it." Yet unless we take the time and effort to organize our closets, our tasks, our rooms, our goals, and our thinking, we'll be like a thousand strips of lumber floating helter-skelter down a river—no plan, no streamlining, no direction. Take the time to nail those pieces of wood into a boat, and you can maneuver rapidly and cleanly through even the worst currents.

In some of my classes we talk a lot about energy and how to best utilize it, not waste it, get more of it, etc. I always think about personal energy, not just oil and solar. So many people spin through life like whirling dervishes, yet they never seem to accomplish anything. At the end of the week they're utterly exhausted, yet they can't point to anything they did. How sad, when with just a little organizing they could use that energy to propel them through life and give them hours of free time as well.

I don't really know if my parents taught me to work hard or not. Once in awhile somebody will give a talk in sacrament meeting, and they'll comment on how grateful they are that their parents made them milk cows and put up fences. I always sit there feeling guilty for living in a city where my major daily task is to make my bed or do light housework. I start to wonder if I've really learned how to work or not.

But I also think it's an attitude, and that if I had to milk cows I could do it. I'm not ashamed just because I don't have to churn butter, after all. I dig into what I'm asked to do, and I can honestly say I don't procrastinate *too* much. But I'll also be first to tell you I don't like work, and I find it completely impossible to relate to a woman who hums while she's vacuuming. I'll vacuum all right, but I'll do it just to get it over with. I like the feeling of a job well done, and I like a clean house. But I do not like scrubbing toilets or washing floorboards, and if you don't like it either, I don't think you should feel bad about it. As long as the job gets done, I think I've conquered enough.

A lot of people think that if they can't love it, there's something wrong with them. Then they get discouraged and they don't do it at all. People sit in sloppy living rooms and moan, "What can I say? I just hate housework." Now that's wrong. Even if we don't like it, that shouldn't keep us from doing any at all.

My dad taught me that actually. He had given up on our poor old garden until all Mortimer was doing was protecting the dirt clods. But last week I noticed Dad was thumbing through a new garden catalog, and I pretended to be stunned and astonished (this didn't take much acting).

"What? Are you actually going to try again?" I sat down beside him, shocked.

Dad chuckled and shook his head. Then he wrinkled his nose and said, "I hate a quitter."

I smiled. I was so proud he had decided not to give up. It made me want to be like that. Dad told me he really was grateful to have enough land to plant a garden and that he was thankful he had good enough health to do the work. He said he owed it to the Lord to try again.

I guess that's what people mean when they say to appreciate work. Just being well enough to do it is exciting. Dad's mother came to stay with us for the summer before she died about five years ago. Grandma Barker was a beautiful lady. She really was, even though she was older than most of my friends' grandmothers and very frail. She had glorious wavy hair that she wore in a braided bun, and sparkling green eyes that formed laughing crescents whenever she talked with me.

She came to stay with us because she'd had a stroke and was paralyzed on one side. We fixed up a bed for her in the guest room, and I helped buy her a giant color TV of her very own. We used to spend hours talking, and sometimes I'd read to her or listen to her stories of "the olden days."

Toward the end she suffered so much that her death was a blessing and a relief. We were sad to see her go and we missed her terribly, but we loved her too much to want her to stay and suffer. Anyway, she helped me learn to appreciate the ability to work because she so desperately missed doing it herself.

She had always been so active; she painted gorgeous landscapes and crocheted intricate sweaters. She even used to tat lacy doilies and pillowcase trimmings. Her handwriting used to be so pretty, just like calligraphy. And she was always one of those industrious cooks who would get up at 5:00 a.m. to put up jam or apricots.

One day I took her lunch in to her, and she knocked over a glass of lemonade and broke it. I hurried in with some paper towels, and Grandma was crying. I kept trying to calm her and assure her that it was an accident and that a broken glass is no big deal. Finally, after she collected herself and dried the tears, she said, "It's only a glass to you, Louisa. To me, it's the loss of everything I know how to do."

To her, that glass was a reminder of her new limitations, and she knew she would never again be as capable as she once was. Right then it hit me how lucky I am to be able to hold a glass and wash dishes and walk up and down stairs and slice my own sandwiches! All the little burdensome tasks and chores suddenly seemed like precious blessings.

We really should appreciate work. We should do high-quality work and give honest efforts. We should be proud of our accomplishments and grateful for the health which lets us earn them. Our accomplishments help us to build confidence, and if we always look for the easy way out, we'll never have the self-esteem we deserve.

Another thing Grandma taught me was to use my leisure time wisely. I used to say, "Oh, Grandma, please. When I have spare time I want to relax and do nothing." But she showed me the difference between rejuvenating and rusting. I now fill my time with sports and play for exercise, reading for mental stimulation, meditation for spirituality, conversation for social growth, hobbies for my own satisfaction and fun, and sleep only when I really need it. I feel just as relaxed, but now I have recreation that means something. I'm getting something out of it instead of throwing my time away.

When I think of things that are hard to do, I don't always think of work in the traditional sense. I think of the tremendous effort it is sometimes just to maintain friendships. And yet a good friend is so valuable it's worth all the effort you can give it. A couple of ideals I try to reach in being a friend are these: First, I remember that we all seem to worry and take care that others don't use us or offend us, yet the ideal is to be exactly the opposite—to be so loving that our main concern is that we do not use or offend others. And the second ideal is to try to leave everyone I touch a little better, a little improved, for having met me. They aren't always easy goals to attain, but just edging towards them makes me feel good.

One of the main keys, I guess, is to do your best in whatever position you find yourself, be it the position of friend or worker. The fastest way to advance is to do your current duty well. Let's say you're a stagehand instead of the prima ballerina in the school production. Okay, then be the best stagehand there ever was. Let's say you're in charge of cleanup at the girls' camp instead of being captain of the rowing team. Okay, then make that camp the cleanest camp ever! It follows in every role you assume. As a sister, a daughter, a student, a Mormon—all the various things we are—we should be the best we can be. The most useless activity I can think of is grumbling, and that's what I want to avoid (Mom would underline this if she were reading it!). But really, grumbling and whining does nothing except annoy everybody around you. The best and most mature thing to do is accept your position or your tasks and then do the best you can with them.

Even though we're young, we can still accomplish a lot. We can work and learn skills and get jobs and, most of all, we can serve others and provide compassionate service that will truly lift somebody's life. Serving others is what the gospel of Christ is all about. And I know a young kid can make a difference. We don't have to wait until we're in Relief Society to take a loaf of bread to someone or offer to watch their children or call to say hello or send a get well card. We can be demonstrating love right now. Really ask yourself what Jesus would do.

I finally finished my "row" of weeds in Heather's garden. Her mom had gone inside to dish up some homemade (ahhhh) ice cream, and the rest of us stuffed weeds into trash bags.

"In heaven it's just the opposite," I said. "The vegetables and flowers take over and grow like crazy, and you have to work to grow weeds."

Heather laughed. "Maybe we need to figure out how to eat these; then we'd never have to do yard work."

Her dad tied some of the sacks and tossed them into a big cart. "Or we could buy a goat, and Heather could train it to eat everything except the vegetables."

Heather shook her head. "Good luck."

We walked wearily toward her backyard, my aching muscles motivated solely by the vision of fresh peach ice cream—homemade. We turned and looked back at the garden, its rich soil dark where we'd pulled up weeds. The corn stalks were sturdy, stretching proudly toward the blazing sun. Crimson tomatoes hung heavily on their stems, juice-filled and sweet.

"That is one good-looking garden," I said. And I resolved right then to dig in (literally) with my dad and get ours to look as nice. It wouldn't be easy, but it would be right.

On the way home (after a second helping of ice cream that was so smooth and glorious I nearly passed out), I walked by the McMansion again. I ducked under some branches and scaled the pile of dirt, gripped the top of a fence and swung a leg over, climbed down the other side, took the path around by the tool shed, and pulled myself up a hill, grabbing rocks and twigs to help myself along.

At the top was the lilac bush, and I collapsed, weary but happy, underneath it.

Mrs. McMurphy came out into her yard and looked up the hill at me. "Louisa, is that you?"

"Hi, Mrs. McMurphy. Mom said your lilacs were in bloom."

"That's right. Aren't they wonderful?"

"Heaven," I called back.

"You climbed way back there just to smell the lilacs?" she asked me.

I glanced back at the way I had come, the obstacle course I had followed to find this bush. It had been a lot of work. I smiled and called back to her. "But it was McWorth it."

MYTH 12

I Have the World's Worst Luck

Ah, yes, glorious self-pity. Everything horrible happens to me. The whole world is dumping on me. Nothing ever goes right. Life is out to get me. Boo, hoo, hoo. The trouble with indulging in self-pity is the same trouble with scratching a mosquito bite; it feels good at first, but it just makes the problem worse.

Bad things happen to everybody. Because it isn't always easy to admit our own hand in our troubles ("I should have called ahead, I guess" or "I didn't think of that" or "I just figured someone else would do it" or "I slept in" or "I forgot"), we blame circumstances, luck, and life in general.

"See? There's *never* a parking spot when I go shopping," Kelly said once.

I smiled and said nothing. But I thought, "Of course not. You wait until the day before Christmas, you wait until five o'clock when everybody's getting off work, and you shop at the busiest mall in the known world."

But rather than admit her poor planning, it was easier for Kelly to believe that the Parking Spaces of America had secretly met and agreed never to be available when Kelly comes rolling by in her Datsun.

I'm not picking on Kelly; we all sometimes rationalize and blame whatever or whomever is handy. And occasionally we look at others whose lives seem to be gliding effortlessly along. We think we are the only ones with illogical parents, untrue boyfriends, tyrannical bosses, vicious teachers, boring wardrobes, oily skin, crooked teeth, and big noses. The entire rest of the world was blessed with perfect profiles, dainty features, piano-key smiles, glamorous clothes, understanding parents, loving boyfriends, smooth complexions, dazzling figures, super jobs, and easy teachers. Only I have been dealt a rotten hand. I am the only one in the universe who suffers such incredible fate.

Sound familiar? And it feels good at first, doesn't it? Just like scratching a mosquito bite. We get to feel nice and sorry for ourselves. We pat ourselves on the back and "there, there" until we have convinced ourselves that we're being picked on and discriminated against. It's not our fault, we say; it's bad luck.

And then we sit for a couple of minutes more, but somehow we don't feel "all better." In fact, we feel worse! Aaugh! Just like an insect bite that's swelling and getting itchier, our self-pity is growing bigger and more painful by the minute.

What can you do? Just stop, that's what. Sometimes you have to wrap a bandage around your arm so you won't scratch that bite, and sometimes you have enough willpower to simply resist the urge. But whatever it takes, you have to stop or you'll face infection and scarring—all kinds of bigger problems. It's the same with self-pity. If we don't stop, we'll end up depressed and miserable and paranoid. All the horrible things we made up to rationalize will actually become true because of our negative stance, our determination to fail in life.

Maybe you can pull yourself out of it with sheer determination. But maybe you need a bandage, and I'll tell you what one to use: service. Get right up out of your pouting chair and dig into something that's useful, something that helps someone else. Don't sit and wallow in your disappointments. Get involved! Get your mind off your worries and onto the task at hand. It doesn't have to be strenuous; it just has to be other-centered.

Count your blessings. Out loud. Think about all the things you have to be grateful for. You can read. You can eat USDA-approved meat, unlike many people of the world who get worms all the time. You can get water out of a faucet instead of from a pond where half the neighborhood washes its clothes and where the cows wade. You have a television. You can carry a tune. You can see. You can hear. You're healthy. You sleep in a clean bed on a mattress. Now I know a lot of these things sound almost ridiculous, but they're the things we take for granted. Do you realize how many people in the world don't have—and never will have—these things? We have no right to sit and whine about our sorry lot in life when we have so much. And the greatest blessing of all is yours: You're a member of the true, restored church of Jesus Christ. Imagine! What are the odds of being so lucky?

I'm not saying we should never feel disappointment. There are setbacks and trials that come into everyone's life, heartbreaks and failures that try our strength. But if we don't take risks and if we avoid any chance of being hurt or facing failure or getting tired, we never develop the traits that will see us through when the going really does get tough. If you never have to be meticulous doing a chore at home, then you'll have a hard time holding a job when the employer expects quality work and you can't deliver it. If you never allow yourself to care about someone who then disappoints you, you'll never learn the kind of selflessness and forgiveness that you need to steer a marriage or raise children. Our trials and setbacks are terrible to suffer through, but they can teach us an awful lot.

I had a boyfriend once named Jeff. I guess he really wasn't a boyfriend because we were in junior high, much too young to date. But we liked each other and we'd walk through the halls together and he held my hand one time during a school assembly. If you're already dating you probably think it sounds silly, but to me it was an important relationship. I mean, I dreamed about Jeff morning, noon, and night. He'd get his brother to drive by my house, and one time I saw him. I was on cloud nine! I called all my girl friends and they all rushed over and we sat glued to the window to see if he'd drive by again. The anticipation was probably as sweet as the moment when he actually did drive by. We all squealed and threw pillows at each other and hurriedly closed the curtains. I lived in mortal fear that he saw me and all my friends' faces pressed up against the window, steaming the entire living room up, waiting for him to reappear.

The next day at school my stomach was full of butterflies and my face probably looked like a neon sign that keeps flashing from red to white, red to white. I couldn't stop blushing every time I thought that maybe Jeff saw us watching for him. Maybe he thinks we were trying to embarrass him; should I apologize? Maybe he thinks I'm desperately in love with him and am chasing him; should I act aloof? I made so much out of it because when you're that age and your feelings of love are just awakening, it seems like the greatest, scariest, most exciting, most heart-wrenching discovery of your life. And to have that first crush *returned* by a boy whose very name makes your heart pound—it was almost more than my little eighth-grade body could take.

I spent hours thinking of names for our children. I had daydreams about us finally being able to go out on a date. I imagined him coming over to do homework sometime. I thought of him sitting in his bedroom (it had to be tastefully masculine with polished wood and thick rugs, I thought) and getting sidetracked from his history homework. Maybe he was dreamily sighing about the name Louisa May Alcott Ziona Barker. Okay, maybe not the whole thing, maybe just the Louisa part.

Various friends of his would point me out to him in the halls and snicker. My friends relayed messages and concerns on his part about whether I liked him or not. We were all so shaky and shy, yet dying to be in real love.

And then it happened: the crushing blow that shattered my little Cinderella castle forever. I went into home ec after school to pick up a sack of my sewing stuff, and there he was in the closet, kissing Amy Van Boring. Her name was really Amy Van Buren, but to make myself feel better after the incident, I renamed her.

I slammed the door on them and ran from the room, down the hall to my locker, frantically spinning the combination and grabbing my books, then out the front doors of the school. I remember my eyes were burning with tears, and everything seemed a watery blur. My legs just ran and ran beneath me, almost of their own will. I don't know when I have felt so devastated, so betrayed.

Sure, looking back it's not as if we had a commitment or even a mature relationship. It was just hesitant smiles and ticklish butterflies and the rumors back and forth that we each liked each other. But I had counted on it. My own fault, absolutely, and I knew that even then. But it still hurt. I still wanted to die and never speak to another male as long as I lived.

I guess at that moment, if someone had told me to count my blessings and be grateful for USDA meat, I'd have hit them in the smacker with my *Rocks and Minerals* book. When you feel like a toad on a railroad track—*after* the train has passed by—you're still a little too dazed to be "thinking happy thoughts."

But even from major disappointments, we can recover. Not only was I able to enjoy life again, but I was even able to look at Jeff and not wince. I came to see him as a dippy little twerp who didn't appreciate a good thing when he had it (not that I would have hidden in the home ec closet with him). And that's another thing: I decided that any guy who'd meet some girl in the home ec closet like that—well, the move speaks for itself, doesn't it?

Looking back, it wasn't such a hot romance I'd had with Jeff. It's just that he was my first flame, and my feelings and fantasies were especially vulnerable at that tender age. In fact, I am now able to look at that experience as a growing one, one that taught me a thing or two about love and romance. I didn't become hardened and cynical, but I did learn the difference between puppy love and the real thing that you build slowly with someone over time. I became a little wiser I think. We all have to learn that.

In the Doctrine and Covenants 122:5-7 it says, "If thou art called to pass through tribulation, . . . know thou . . . that all these things shall give thee experience, and shall be for thy good." Of course Heavenly Father never sends misfortune to anybody. And he probably winces when he sees some of his children beset by so many problems. But he does give us the ability to handle what comes our way. And he gave us prayer so we could ask for his help. We shouldn't pray to be relieved of all hardships; we should pray for the traits we will need to sail through them.

And since we are to thank God in all things, we should thank him for the opportunity to learn and grow from each difficulty. If you can always learn something from each experience, however painful that experience is, then you'll never take a step back; you'll just keep growing and learning and pushing upward.

Enduring to the end is as hard as anything I can think of. It means staying absolutely true and holding fast to the iron rod, right up until God says you've made it. I heard a fireside speaker say that "the end" even goes beyond death! (Of course, I'm only going to worry about this life for right now; that's a big enough job right there!) But we need to make ourselves a promise that we won't be quitters, that we won't give up. God won't allow us to have bigger trials or greater temptations than he knows we can bear. When these things come your way, just reach out to him and say, "I am going to do my absolute best." And he'll reach back and help you reach the goal. I know he will.

Sometimes horrible things happen to us and we think we will never recover. A girl becomes an unwed mother. A boy loses his father. Parents get a divorce. A guy gets sent home from his mission. A girl is kicked out of school for cheating. A man is fired just before he retires and receives no benefits. A hundred other horrible things happen to people and they think, "This is it; this is the bottom. I will never climb out."

But we have to believe that we can overcome and can attain our potential anyway. Heavenly Father will never let you be in such a terrible spot that you can't grow or learn. You could become a blind and deaf paraplegic tomorrow, and there could still be beauty in life for you. As long as you can learn something new and as long as you can give something to others—if just your love and a caring heart—your life will have great meaning. There's never an excuse for wallowing in self-pity and thinking life is not worth living.

George Matthew Adams once said, "It is no disgrace to start all over. It is usually an opportunity." And throughout your life you'll meet lots of people (even more if you look for them) who are in a happy, productive position because of an earlier setback. "If Eric hadn't walked out on me and gotten a divorce I might never have met John," a bride will say. Yet when Eric first left she probably felt devastated.

"If IBM hadn't fired me, I might never have gotten a job with Xerox," some man will say, thrilled at the new opportunities before him. Yet when he was first fired he probably felt crushed.

"If I hadn't had such terrible acne I might never have developed my sense of humor and my personality," said a girl whom I actually heard when she was talking about skin care on the radio. Here she was, suffering from a disfiguring handicap that makes a lot of people retreat into a shell, but she was using it to grow. Her stumbling block literally had become a stepping stone.

It even works on a small scale. I wanted to take an art class one semester, but there was a waiting list and I didn't make it. My mom tried to console me and said she thought a foreign language would be nice. I groaned; art would be a lot more fun I thought. But I signed up for Spanish, and three surprise benefits resulted. One was that I learned enough to talk about the gospel when I meet a Spanish-speaking person (which is quite frequent in Los Angeles). Another is that I later found out I need foreign language for admittance to UCLA and some other good schools, and I just about blew my chance. And the last is that the art class turned out to be a real joke. The teacher had parties at his house all the time and really promoted a free-wheeling, drug-oriented life-style that I'm glad I don't have to put up with now. If I had been able to take the class, I'd have been much worse off.

Sometimes we don't see such immediate benefits to our initial disappointments and sorrows. Sometimes we have to suffer a long time, and sometimes we never do realize how it was to our advantage. But we have to be patient and watch for our strengths to develop over time. If nothing else, trials teach us patience.

Dr. M. Lynn Bennion once said, "Religion does not teach us everything at once. It does not clear up all our difficulties. Some religious teachers have seemed to think that it is a reproach to religion not to be able to give a categorical answer to every question. They make assertions where the wise and reverent person often will be silent or recognize his lack of insight. There are many things which still are wrapped in wonder, and many ways in which we see God not fully but only in glimpses, like sunshine through the clouds."

I like that quote because it talks about how one can gradually gain a testimony and slowly learn the truths of the gospel as one is ready. But I also like it because it talks about patience in general. We don't always know why we have to do things which are difficult, whether it's enduring the death of a loved one or tackling a hard physical project. But we persevere and ultimately the blessings do come.

Henry David Thoreau said, "Did you ever hear of a man who had striven all his life faithfully and singly toward an object and in no measure obtained it? If a man constantly aspires, is he not elevated?" And you know, it's true. If you want something desperately enough, you'll get it. (Just make sure you really do want it!) Even making progress *toward* a goal is satisfying.

Occasionally we find ourselves in situations where we have to accept change. Let's say you have to skip college and work to support younger brothers and sisters. Or maybe your family moves to an area where you have to shovel snow nine months out of the year. Or your ailing aunt comes to live with your family, and you have to adjust to her health problems. So many things can happen to us all, and the people who best survive these occurrences are the ones who can accept change. Instead of beating their heads against the wall and saying, "But I don't *want* to have my house be burned down," we sometimes have to look at the reality and just accept it. The house is in ashes; those are the facts. The best thing to do is accept whatever problem has arisen, realize you can't wish it away, and then do what you can to cope. We'll all face disappointments. We have to get back up and keep working. People who say, "If it's not easy, forget it" will crumple up like a dead leaf at the slightest ripple of a breeze. They won't be able to handle the weather. We simply must accept change.

Sometimes we get a distorted picture of what a trial really is. We think because we're teased at school that the whole world is horrible. We think because we have to vacuum and do dishes that we're nothing more than legal slaves. I think it's good to count our blessings and realize that we have it better than any generation ever had it before. And in the United States, anyway, we have a life-style that is beyond the dreams of a starving baby in Africa or a begging mother in India. We put better food down our disposals than most of the world ever get to eat. I look back at the pioneers and what they went through, losing their loved ones and burying them in the frozen ground along the way, leaving their beautiful homes, lugging their wagons across the plains and up steep mountains. They're a pretty spectacular bunch of people (even if one of them *did* invent the name *Ziona*). How humbling it is to know how they suffered and still imagine them singing, "And should we die before our journey's through, Happy day! all is well! We then are free from toil and sorrow, too; With the just we shall dwell! But if our lives are spared again To see the Saints their rest obtain, O how we'll make this chorus swell—All is well! all is well!"

Lots of members and many Church leaders have said that we have it just as hard today as they had in pioneer times, but that instead of physical tribulations, our test is one of ease and comfort. We have so many material things and life is so automated, so simplified, that our idle time gets filled with greed, lust, jealousy, conceit, and all those other evils that the pioneers never had time for. They may have struggled harder against nature's elements, but we struggle harder against the "natural man" within.

Just the fact that we have time to feel sorry for ourselves periodically ought to tell us we have too much time on our hands. When we're busy accomplishing good works or doing kind deeds for others, our own lives seem happier and we have less time to sit around and listen to knocks in the engine.

There's another reason why our lives seem better and happier and luckier when we're serving; do you want to know what it is?

It's because they *are*.

MYTH 13

As Long As Nobody Finds Out, So What?

Remember Kelly's sister, Rebecca—the one who's "sort of engaged" to a third of the population in the Western Hemisphere? (while her boyfriend Mitch is being groomed to be my eternal companion, I hope, I hope). Well, she went over to Mitch's house last April and told Mitch's mother that as long as she and Mitch were probably going to end up together, she might just as well have Mitch's conference tapes. Mitch's mother trusts anybody, which is a good trait to have until you're about thirteen or so, and she gave Rebecca the tapes.

So then Rebecca ran home and was giggling to Kelly and me that she wasn't going to give the tapes back, ever, even if they broke up. Can you imagine? What could be more ironic than stealing conference tapes? Stealing Bibles, maybe. It's like forging a temple recommend or paying your tithing with Monopoly money. It has to be the height of *something*.

And poor Mitch worked so hard to be able to buy a videotape recorder, just so he could have a complete collection of all the conference tapes and some ball games and other things he wanted to save. Needless to say, Kelly's dad made Rebecca take them back, but she only did so under great duress.

Her biggest regret was that she had told Kelly and that Kelly had "tattletaled." Rebecca's like a lot of crooks who are very sorry—sorry they got caught, that is.

Honesty and integrity are things you learn informally. You can't take a class in ethics that will turn you into a law-abiding citizen who never again scoots past a stop sign, even though you always did before. It's something you've internalized early and usually from observing the examples of those around you. It's a determination to adhere consistently to moral values, never wavering. It's an inner light of strength and a sense of obligation to stay true to the finest code of living we know. And let's face it: We all know what's noblest and best. We all know how we really should behave. But it takes courage to live it.

We talked about this in Sunday School one week. Our teacher wrote this on the board: "The measure of a man's real character is what he would do if he knew he never would be found out." Thomas Babington Macaulay said that over a century ago, and our teacher asked us what we thought about it.

Some of the kids thought that if no one knew what you were doing that anything you wanted to do was okay. But it soon became clear to us that whether you get caught or not is completely beside the point. It's doing what's right even when you're all alone.

We had a substitute teacher in algebra who taught me a lot more than math. Mr. Braemar came to replace Miss Gault, who in telling us she was going to have a baby, made up the most ridiculous joke about a watermelon patch and swallowing the seed, etc. that you ever heard. Needless to say, Miss Gault might have done well to pop in on our health class occasionally.

But anyway, Mr. Braemar used to leave the room during tests. I mean, he'd hand them out and then actually leave for the rest of the period. "Put them on the desk when you're through," he'd say. We were stunned. We all just sat there the first time and watched him walk out. Was he actually leaving us alone, giving us the freedom to cheat or throw paper airplanes or dance on the desks? We all just sat there for a minute.

And then a strange thing happened. Maybe it wouldn't have worked in another school, or maybe another teacher wouldn't have won our loyalty the way Mr. Braemar had, but we all just quietly took our tests and resisted the urge to glance at our neighbor's paper. We were on the honor system, and we chose to have integrity. I remember nearly every question on that test, and I remember I got a pretty decent grade on it. I have never been so proud of a test score in my life, even though I've done better and have refrained from cheating before and after Mr. Braemar's class.

What made me so proud of myself is that I had the freedom to cheat without punishment, and I chose, of my own free will, to be honest. I proved to myself that I can do it and be strong, even if no teacher is suspiciously glaring at us all.

You can accuse me of stretching a real-life incident in order to get an object lesson out of it, but I tell you, I found myself comparing Mr. Braemar's class to the final judgment. (So did some of the kids who hadn't studied or kept up, now that I think about it!) But you know this: There are no angels following us around and tapping us on the shoulder every time we blow it in this life. No heavenly messengers strong-arm us out of some guy's back seat, and nobody pulls that cigarette out of our fingers if we're determined to break commandments. We have our free agency, and we choose to be righteous all on our own. Forced compliance was Satan's way, after all. (By the way, I tried to convince my parents that Mr. Braemar was following God's plan and that any other method of testing was Satanic, and I didn't get very far. Just so you don't try to do the same.)

But again, it's harder to be honest if you know you're not being monitored. Yet we all want to attain greatness. If you walked up to someone—anyone—on the street and said, "Would you like to be mediocre?" they'd say, "Of course not." (Well, first they might wonder who you were and why it was any of your business.) But seriously, nobody wants to fail to reach their potential. We all want to develop as many good traits as we can. The trouble is, few of us want to work hard enough to do that.

To be really great, you have to put integrity ahead of selling out and doing what the rest of the world seems to be doing. Just because everybody else is doing it, doesn't make it the right thing to do.

It really is hard these days to attain true greatness. It's much more difficult than being great in the worldly sense (a great ballplayer, a great salesman, a great singer) because there are no trophies, no financial rewards, no autograph seekers, and no applause when someone develops great character. There are no arenas wherein this is specifically rewarded. It's so much easier to get sidetracked and become great at something everyone will rave about.

Here's what President Joseph F. Smith said about that: "Those things which we call extraordinary, remarkable, or unusual may make history, but they do not make real life.

"After all, to do well those things which God ordained to be the common lot of all mankind, is the truest greatness. To be a successful father or a successful mother is greater than to be a successful general or a successful statesman. . . . It is true that such secondary greatness may be added to that which we style common-place; but when such secondary greatness is not added to that which is fundamental, it is merely an empty honor."

It's so tempting to be the total career woman. A lot of my friends don't ever want to get married or have children; they want to be tycoons or accomplished violinists or jet-setting socialites. They want to excel at the things that matter least. They want to be millionaires more than they want to be mothers. They are gladly willing to sacrifice the one thing that can bring them the most satisfaction: the family. And they're afraid that if they stop to marry and have children, they'll lose their sense of self. I guess they look at frazzled women with three toddlers who watch soap operas and get fat and never read or visit a museum and who don't develop any talents and who only grumble about diapers and cooking all day. These women would have been just as miserable without kids, you know. They'd be the grouchy secretaries who sigh like it will kill them if their boss asks them to sharpen a pencil. They'd be just as fat and lazy in any other role because that's how they are. But if you're dynamic and ambitious and energetic in your work, then you'll take these same traits into marriage and parenting, and you'll find you have loads of time to develop other interests and be mentally stimulated. I've talked with a lot of my friend's moms and sisters about this, and I honestly believe it. Put the family first, and God will see that you feel fulfilled. You'll find time to do the other things you enjoy, too.

You'll have the contentment of one who has been given higher information, one who operates with greater knowledge. And in staying true to that, in having integrity and conviction, you'll become truly great.

Integrity is a funny thing to think about when you're on a date, but it has a lot to do with chastity. When we give in to physical urges that cause us to break God's commandments, we're not staying true to the finest living code we know; we're buckling under and choosing to fail. How sad, when Heavenly Father wants nothing more than for us to return home to him, and he's right there waiting to help us, but we ignore him.

The title of this chapter, "As Long As Nobody Finds Out, So What?" is a direct quote from a guy I dated, and it was his closing line. I mean, he hadn't meant it to be his closing line, but I arranged that for him anyway. He was determined to wear me down and get me to relax my standards. I kept telling him that I didn't want to have to tell my bishop about my dates and that a goodnight kiss was a more than generous way to end the evening.

"Your bishop doesn't have to know," he said. "Just don't tell him."

I looked at him incredulously and said, "But *I* would know!" And then he delivered this chapter's title. So, if he wasn't good for much else, at least that guy helped me finish this book! But seriously, it is completely beside the point, whether you "tell" or not. *You* know what you do and whether you are living God's commandments. Being a coward and committing moral sins without confessing them to the bishop (who is really only acting as the Lord's representative and doing what God would have him do) doesn't mean you're off the hook. It only means you'll have to answer to the Lord someday, probably after it's too late to make corrections.

I'll be honest. Chastity is my biggest challenge, and it isn't always as easy for me to say no as I made it sound just now. I really struggle to keep high standards (higher ones than a lot of girls keep, simply because I know how very weak I am). I'm not one who can court disaster and not fall off the edge. Once I am let loose in a bakery, I'm afraid I'd gobble up everything in sight, you know? So I don't even wander in to begin with. I stay plenty clear of the temptations, and I think we all should. It's too frustrating and difficult to promise ourselves we'll "be good" and then plant ourselves in dangerous situations that seem designed to get us to surrender our virtue. I'm talking about the kinds of seemingly innocent activities that tend to go too far: parking "to talk" after a date, watching TV alone at his house while his parents are out, dates that last too long (when you run out of things to do, it's easy to think of sex as the next activity), dates that begin too late in the evening (which means you'll be spending too many late-night hours together, and you know as well as I do that temptations are a lot stronger when it's darker and later), and dates with nonmembers.

And also I try not to fantasize about the guy too much. Seriously! When I'm not with him, I try not to wander dreamily around the house imagining what it would be like to kiss him for several hours straight. And I try not to relive all the wonderful things he says or the way candlelight enhances his rugged features. I don't kid myself into thinking I'm not attracted to him; I face the fact that I am. But I don't let myself get carried away in a steamy or fanciful daydream. Our bishop gave a youth fireside once and said that every act of immorality began as a simple thought. If we can avoid thinking about it, we can avoid doing it.

I guess the best way to tackle this great temptation is deciding beforehand what your standards are and where you'll stop. In Sunday School a few years ago they told a story that I'll always remember. It was about a train engineer. He was speeding along the tracks through a canyon and came up over a hill. Then just like a roller coaster he went charging down the other side toward the valley below. Suddenly the engineer saw a huge pile of lumber on the track, right at the bottom of the hill. Instantly he accelerated and zoomed full speed ahead, bursting through the debris and scattering it like toothpicks as he crashed through it. The train sustained some damage, but no one was injured.

Later the man was commended for his incredible wisdom and quick reaction. If he had slammed on the brakes or tried to slow down, the train would have smacked into the logs and several people would have died; nearly everyone would have been hurt. The train might have leaped the tracks and a terrible tragedy would have resulted. The only decision that saved the passengers was to go even faster and break through the blockade. Yet who, upon seeing such an obstacle ahead, wouldn't want to first try to stop and avoid the situation? I think just about everyone's first reaction would be to hit the brakes.

Someone asked the engineer how he made the right choice so quickly. He said, "I didn't make any choice at all. I had thought about this situation many times before, and I had decided ahead of time what I would do if it ever happened. So when it finally did, I didn't have to think; my choice had simply become a reflex."

That's how we need to be when it comes to sex. We need to decide ahead of time what we'll do and how we'll say no. That way, when the lights are low and the hormones are high, we won't have to weigh the alternatives and make a choice when our judgment is cloudy. We'll already know what to do, and we won't have to think. It will all be automatic.

We're all so young to be confronted with such big decisions in life. I think about my Grandma Barker and how it was when she was dating. Now I know that kids got into trouble in those days, too, but sexual experimentation wasn't anything like it is today. If a girl said no, a guy not only respected it, but he would have been stunned if she'd said anything else! Today we have to defend and give reasons and put up with an eager date whose sole objective is to wear us down and get us to give in.

In fact, I've even dated guys who say that nearly every girl they date is the first one to suggest it! Can you imagine? But I'll tell you this: They confide that to me after I've said no, and they tell me how refreshing it is to meet a girl with morals for a change. They really do; I can see their eyes light up, and suddenly they realize they're out with someone who can be their friend, someone they can open up with and share honest feelings. I can't tell you how many guys have told me that they're sick of overly aggressive women who nearly tear their clothes off on the first date. Winning a guy's respect is important to me, and I know that by holding fast to my convictions I can do it.

Anyway, I hadn't really planned to say much about dating; it opens up a whole new can of worms (and I've dated most of them). But I know staying morally clean is the hardest thing of all for *this* Louisa May Alcott, and we can't give up just because it isn't easy.

Let's do something. I mean it. Let's all promise ourselves to hang onto our virtue. Let's really fast and pray for strength, and then let's really make a commitment. It's so easy to slip, to rationalize behaving like all those seemingly happy-go-lucky people around us. Before you know it, criticisms of the Church creep in, and behavior that you thought was only straying a tiny bit from the center will pull you completely away from all the blessings God wants to give you.

It might be hard, but if we hang in there it will be worth it. We'll have blessings in this life, not just in the hereafter. We'll be productive, happy citizens, happily married lovers, terrific moms, and dynamite women. All because we learned when we were young that doing what's right, even when it's hard, is the true road to happiness.

A couple of months ago my mom tacked a quote onto the refrigerator, specifically onto the freezer door, which houses the ice cream cache which she knew Dad and I would be sure to see. It was by Elder J. Thomas Fyans, and it said, "Living the gospel is like combing your hair. No matter how well you did it yesterday you must do it again today."

It was clever and I chuckled. But the longer I thought about it, the more profound it sounded. We really have to work on our testimonies every single day, or they begin to wither and die.

Having integrity and doing what's right—even if nobody else knows— takes daily effort and *conscious* effort. We all know our weaknesses, and we need to have especially tight reigns on them.

And anyway, it's impossible that "nobody finds out" because of course God will know. And you yourself will know.

And you are not a nobody.

MYTH 14

I Can't Help It; This Is Just the Way I Am

Baloney. I mean, excuse me for beginning a chapter so abruptly, but I really have to quarrel with the notion that we can't change, that our dispositions are set in cement.

Anyone can change *if they want to*. They really can. But if you aren't miserable enough with a certain aspect of your personality, if you aren't motivated strongly enough to change it, you'll never conquer it.

For example, Mom keeps telling me to relax about makeup and clothes. And I know in my heart that she's right, that the outward ornaments don't make the person. But I need to be motivated from the inside before I can let go of these hang-ups. I wouldn't even say they're hang-ups; I'd just say my priorities need a little untangling. But until I decide that I don't like being that way, I'll probably stay the same.

Barbara talked to me about it once. She said that one day I'll be shopping or ironing and I'll look at the kinds of clothes I'm buying and I'll say, "Good grief, this looks like something a dumb little kid would wear." And suddenly my wardrobe will take on a more sophisticated, classic style and not be full of so many wacky fad items.

She said that one day I'll look in the mirror and I'll like myself so much that I won't have to spend all kinds of time primping and fussing with my face.

I'm sure she's right. One day it will hit me that the things which used to be important just aren't anymore. And when that happens (and *only* then, I tell Mom), I will "put aside childish things" and act more responsibly and spend my money more wisely.

But I know I will change. (I *hope* I'll change!) And I look forward to all the growth and development that lies ahead for me. I really believe we can all become whatever we want, and none of us are forced to stay any certain way just because "that's the way I am" or so we think.

We all can—and should—change. An old Hindu proverb says, "There is nothing noble in being superior to some other man. The true nobility is in being superior to your previous self."

A lot of people don't change because they don't feel they're responsible for how they turn out. They feel their environment or their genes determine everything. That's why you find fat families, underachieving families, and people who wallow in the poor circumstances into which they were born—they don't believe they can pull themselves out. But they can!

Not only can we rise to whatever level we choose—in character development, happiness, whatever—but we *should* rise. We *should* take responsibility for how we feel and what we do with our lives. Nobody forces you to fail. If you fail, you do so of your own free will. It's the same with embarrassment or shame: No one can *make* you feel any way except the way you *permit* them to make you feel. Your permission is the key to everything. It's the same with success; when good things happen to you, don't just shrug it off or discount your efforts which helped you succeed. Don't say, "Well, I just got lucky," or "Next time I'll probably blow it." Realize that God has a hand in your achievements and joys, and give him credit. And then give yourself credit, too. If you worked hard to win that blue ribbon, enjoy the fruits of your own labors and realize that you worked and practiced and sacrificed and *that's* why you won—not just because good fortune fell upon you.

We all need to realize that we are in the driver's seat. We can refuse to believe that, we can walk to the back of the bus, we can lie down on the seat and fall asleep if we want to, but no one else is going to steer for you. You, and you alone, are in charge of your life. If you want all the goodies and blessings, then do what you must to earn them. You won't be deprived of happiness if you're serving others and loving your fellowman. Likewise, you won't be blessed with peace of mind or contentment if you're bulldozing through life without any concern for others, if you're selfish or dishonest.

I went out with a guy once who took me home to meet his family at the end of the date. His folks, who claimed to be members of the Church, were drinking coffee, and his dad had on a T-shirt with a crude slogan on the front. Both of them were overweight and wearing short cutoffs. The mother had a couple of rollers in her hair.

I was polite and they seemed cordial, but there wasn't much love or warmth in their home. The TV was blaring, and no one seemed to be talking much with anybody else.

On the way home my date said, "Yeah, my dad says I can go into his business if I want after high school. I'm thinking about it."

"Would you like that kind of work?" I said. It was honest work for a big air conditioning company.

"Sure. I figure if I can do as well as my dad, that's good enough for me. They never got married in the temple, but they're good people and it's a good life."

I sat there, trying to nod or even squeak out a "hmmm," but all I could feel was panic. Panic for me, lest I fall in love with this guy, and panic for him, lest he miss all the joy that a family can be and all the joy of being active in the Church and worthy to enter the temple! He was prepared to settle for so little! All he was thinking of was making a decent living.

That night I looked up something I remembered that President Brigham Young had said, and I thought I'd share it with you: "You may say to yourselves, 'If I can do as well as my parents, I think I shall do well, and be as good as I want to be, and I should not strive to excel them.' But if you do your duty you will far excel them in everything that is good—in holiness, in physical and intellectual strength, for this is your privilege, and it becomes your duty."

Even if we have super parents, we have the duty to become even better, even stronger. We shouldn't hesitate to rise above any level we formerly thought was the ceiling.

We can ease other's burdens and grow in ways we can't even imagine. Serving those around us is, from what limited experience I've had so far, the fastest way to grow up and mature. It's also the fastest way to find true happiness. And for somebody who's as impatient as I am, it's hard to find anything that gives such fast, positive results.

We *can* help how we are, and we owe it to ourselves to make whatever changes we must in order to return to Heavenly Father. I have loads of weaknesses and faults, but I know that I can work with God to overcome them. And I know that if I can do it, anybody can. We can change if we really want to.

We should sit down with a pencil and paper and write up all the goals we can think of. Make a new page for each category: spiritual, mental, social, emotional, physical, financial—any other categories you like. Then list long-term and short-term goals. Write down everything you want in a marriage partner. Make written promises to yourself, and then check the list every month to see how you're doing. If we can plan ahead and then "not flub it" as Kelly might say, we can achieve any level of success we want. But we have to stay true to our standards.

We also need to let our patriarchal blessings guide us along. Those blessings aren't just a list of "fortunes," you know. You're given warnings and advice, too. God tells you some trouble spots to watch out for, and he tells you some special qualities you've been given that will see you through. And then *after* you've been an obedient servant and a true follower of Christ, he tells you the blessings you'll receive. I really cherish my blessing. Whenever I'm down, I get it out and I think, "See? God really does love me!" And I know that he loves you, too.

Avoid costly mistakes that you see your friends making. Don't experiment with sex or drugs—you'd be better off having explosives for a hobby. Don't think that just because you're young you can mess up and you won't have to pay for it later. Everything you are doing today is preparing the way you will go tomorrow.

I've watched so many kids with strong morals and high goals, who go on to attain great success and satisfaction, just by continuing the momentum they built while they were in their teens. And I've also watched others fall behind to fool around, thinking they'll be able to catch up later—only they never do.

I want to be in that first group. I want to bolt off the line right as the shot is fired and run the best race of my life, giving it everything I've got. Life can be a joy and a thrill. It can get better and better every year because *we* can get better and better. No one else is steering your ship. You alone will determine what you do with your life, with your *self*. You can make any changes you want to.

Is there life after youth? You'd better believe there is! And the way you spend your youth will determine what kind of life that might be.

SOURCES CITED

Adams, George Matthew. In *Light from Many Lamps*. Edited by Lillian Eichler Watson. New York: Simon and Schuster, 1951, p. 159.

Bennion, M. Lynn. "Creative Teaching." *Improvement Era*, Nov. 1946, p. 705.

Burton, Theodore M. "The Word of Wisdom." *Ensign*, May 1976, pp. 28-29.

Hindu Proverb. In *Light from Many Lamps*. Edited by Lillian Eichler Watson. New York: Simon and Schuster, 1951, p. 161.

Kimball, Spencer W. "Privileges and Responsibilities of Sisters." *Ensign*, Nov. 1978, p. 105.

————. Unpublished Address. Church Historical Department. Cited in *Testimony*. Compiled by H. Stephen Stoker and Joseph C. Murren. Salt Lake City: Bookcraft, 1980, p. 163.

La Rochefoucauld, Duc De. *Reflections*, no 378. Cited in John Bartlett's *Familiar Quotations*. 14th ed. Edited by Emily Morison Beck. Boston: Little, Brown, and Co., 1968, p. 356.

Lee, Harold B. "Understanding Who We Are Brings Self-Respect." *Ensign*, Jan. 1974, p. 4.

McKay, David O. "The Greatest Possession." *Instructor*, Apr. 1964, p. 129.

Rector, Hartman, Jr. "The World's Greatest Need." *Ensign*, Nov. 1975, p. 11.

Smith, Joseph F. *Juvenile Instructor* 40 (Dec. 1905):752-53.

Taylor, John. In *Journal of Discourses* 12:22; 23:262.

Thoreau, Henry David. In *Light from Many Lamps*. Edited by Lillian Eichler Watson. New York: Simon and Schuster, 1951, p. 141.

Whitney, Orson F. *Millennial Star*, 7 Jan. 1889, p. 2.

Widtsoe, John A. *Evidences and Reconciliations*. 3 vols. in 1. Arranged by G. Homer Durham. Salt Lake City: Bookcraft, 1960, pp. 16-17.

Young, Brigham. *Discourses of Brigham Young*. Compiled by John A. Widtsoe. Salt Lake City: Deseret Book Co., 1954, pp. 202-3.